CW00343030

Contents

Once upon a time...

...in Gilesgate, a spark of an idea came to life.

Books are fun. A good story always stirs something inside of us. Children of all abilities are capable of the most fantastic creations when given time and freedom to imagine.

In a world of SATs, league tables and electronic distractions maybe people on all sides need reminding that story-telling is fun, and important.

This idea starts, as so many stories start, with a thought:

"I wonder if...

Welcome to the Gilesgate Story Challenge, Volume 3.

Foreword

By Simon Berry

We're back! Welcome to the third Gilesgate Story Challenge. Now we are officially a trilogy.

For those of you who don't know about us - where have you been? You should immediately go online and buy all the previous years' books!

The Gilesgate Story Challenge is a short story competition for children. We want to make writing fun and accessible. Our aim is to encourage the wonderful imagination of our authors and not worry too much about how they choose to tell their story. We don't correct grammar and we don't edit their words.

This year we asked for stories related to British Wildlife with all the proceeds of our book going to the Durham Wildlife Trust.

Whatever money you spent on the book you are holding in your hands, you are supporting a local charity. (That means if you are reading someone else's copy you should also go online and donate some money to the Durham Wildlife Trust - tell them we sent you!)

This year we are lucky enough to be joined by guest judges Jenny Pearson and Fiona Sharp. Jenny is a successful children's author and Fiona works in Waterstones, and also runs an independent book review website. I am so pleased to have had their input and expertise.

But, I have to admit to being a little worried about the subject of this year competition. British Wildlife seemed a subject a little too comfortable and familiar. A little too tempting for our authors to write a sequel to Wind in the Willows, or The Gruffalo thinly disguised.

How wrong I was. The children of Durham are amazingly talented and there are some incredible original stories waiting for you between the pages of this book. Any droplet of doubt soon evaporates when you read our first tale. The hero from our winning story is a slug! What a great, original character to have dreamt up.

You are going to read about bullfinches warning rainbow trout, harvest mice that think they are dragons, ladybirds and spiders working together to repair bug houses and animals living in mushrooms… "get it? Mush-rooms."

We've got detective stories, ghost stories, fantasy stories, adventure stories. Some will make you sad, some you will burst out laughing.

A few of these stories have a serious environmental message for us grown-ups, which I guess is not surprising. The authors in this book are from the generation that are going to have to live with the choices that us adults make today and maybe we deserve every little nudge to get us to live more sustainably.

If there was one message to single out, for me it is the "Twisted Meadow" story. It is so vividly described that I can't get out of my head the image of the deer with an "odd look, a look of anger and hatred." I think we are all starting to realise that humans can't just exploit the natural world and walk away from the consequences.

But let us not get too depressing because that is not what this book is all about. These stories remind us that we have an amazing diversity of wildlife in Britain. We should get out and start appreciating that. Find out about the slugs and the bugs, all the wonderful creatures that grace our natural landscapes.

A perfect place to start doing that is by visiting Durham Wildlife Trust. They have 37 nature reserves scattered around the County with plenty to explore. They have all the wildlife habitats covered - wetlands, shoreline, heathland, woodland. It's all there and being preserved by the work they do.

Maybe you can take this book with you on your adventure, but for goodness sake keep it safe. Douglas Adams had a short story published in "The Eagle" when he was aged 12. Terry Pratchett was first published in his school magazine aged 14. With the scale of imagination displayed within these pages, we just might just have another famous author in our midst.

Enjoy these stories, and thanks again for supporting the Gilesgate Story Challenge.

Winning Entry

Sammy the Useful Slug

By Lauren Cumming
Age 11

Sammy was a slug. A brown ordinary slug who thought he had no purpose.

Everyone thought slugs were not useful. What do slugs do?

Sammy was sad that he was a slug. He wished he was a useful animal that people loved.

One day Sammy woke up and decided that he would discover something useful about slugs.

Sammy was feeling excited for the first time ever! He didn't know anything useful about slugs and today he would.

He hoped someone knew something.

In a few minutes time Sammy had reached Rosy Rabbit's burrow. It took him a while to get there as slugs move very slowly.

Sammy asked Rosy if she knew anything useful about slugs.

Rosy brutally said "slugs are not useful, Sammy, you should know that."

Sammy sighed and wriggled away, leaving a slime trail outside of Rosy's burrow. *Maybe Susie sheep knows something,* Sammy thought.

A few moments later, Sammy was at the field where Susie was. There were a lot of sheep there which made it hard to spot Susie.

Susie came up to Sammy and wondered, *why is a useless, tiny slug in a huge, dangerous field like this?*

Sammy asked Susie if she knew anything useful about slugs.

Susie said "All I know is that slugs have green blood, and that's not useful! *Baaa*!" And then she walked away.

Maybe Cally the Cow knows something useful about slugs.

Sammy crossed the field to find Cally, luckily she was next to the fence.

Soon, Sammy asked Cally if she knew anything useful about slugs.

Cally said "No, I don't. Sorry Sammy." Then Cally went to eat some grass.

"There is no point. Slugs are not interesting and I give up!" screamed Sammy.

Then the wise old slug came up to Sammy and said "slugs are actually very useful. We provide food for all sorts of mammals, slow worms, earthworms, insects and they are part of the natural balance.

"So you see, Sammy, slugs are very useful, in fact without slugs, birds especially would have a food shortage."

Sammy was so happy that he'd finally found something useful about slugs.

Most of all he was so grateful that the wise old slug told him all of this. Sammy got the wise old slug a gift.

Tender leaves!

Joint Second Place

The Bug Recyclers

By Hanna Tate
Age 9

One summer's evening, in a busy park, a family laid down their sapphire, checked picnic blanket and made themselves comfortable. Peeking around a mushroom with marshmallow coloured spots was a secret, ruby-red ladybird called Daphne.

Daphne was part of Bug HQ which helps all bugs feel happy because some humans leave their litter everywhere and this fills the bugs' homes with plastic and waste.

The family didn't notice as Daphne scuttled around the picnic blanket collecting crumbs of biscuits, sandwiches, fairy cakes, crisps and lots of other stuff too.

She was collecting that stuff for Bug HQ.

Daphne the ladybird collected the things, Sally the spider put her super sticky spiderwebs around them, and Beatrice the beetle sticks them together.

They were making a home for Old Lady Pink the worm; she came every week because the birds kept pecking her house down.

They usually made the walls out of biscuits, the curtains out of leaves from a birch tree, the roof made from grass and mud. The windows were made out of broken glass left lying around the swings in the park. But unfortunately Daphne couldn't hold it all, and she could only get bread.

Sometime later, a human called Sarah who loves bugs picked up Daphne and put her in a warm shelter with a wooden sign. Carved into it was 'Bug Hotel'.

Meanwhile, Old Lady Pink was trying to

flee her house. The birds were even more hungry than usual. They were looking at Old Lady Pink with their beady eyes…

She was going to be eaten!

Daphne saw the whole thing so she quickly scuttled to Old Lady Pink and took her to the Bug Hotel with Sarah. Daphne took her there because it was safe, healthy and not polluted.

And Daphne kept on helping people and seeing her friends in Bug HQ.

D Is for Detecting

By Finja Weinzierl
Aged 9

Fern darted through the trees, her fox tail trailing behind and a stitch eating away at her side but she didn't stop running. A detective was never, ever late, but here she was running through the trees, late for her own cousin's Mehndi* party!

When she arrived eight minutes late, she couldn't help feeling relieved. At least she wasn't that late, and no-one seemed to notice! I guess there were so many people there that Dawn – her cousin – couldn't keep track of all the guests. Suddenly there was an announcement.

The voice sounded urgent, so Fern pricked her ears to listen.

"All guests must stay in this room. The police will come over in a minute to ask you all about a theft that has happened next door. A priceless crown has been stolen from the museum.

Dawn jumped up, smudging one of her mehndi patterns, and cried "what?!"

Fern's nose flicked up in the air. This was a crime! This was what she had been waiting for! She was going to solve it!

She ran to the door. But her dad leaped in front of her. Wagging his front paw at her, he said "uh-uh-uh. Where do you think you're going, missy? This is your cousin's mehndi party, and you are staying right here. Also, the police said we need to stay in this room!"

"But this will help me become the world's greatest detective, dad!"

"You're staying right here. Now, that's the police's orders."

"Uhhhhh…" said Fern, turning around to go back to the food banquet. But she didn't give up; she would get away. She had to.

After two more attempts in which she was caught – once by her mum, and once by her aunty – she finally made it out of the hall. She ran along the garden path, making her way to the museum. When there, she stood marvelling at the big tall building. OK, it was time for detecting! She scurried inside, eager to solve the mystery.

20 minutes later...

In books, they made detecting sound easy. But it wasn't. She had been looking for clues for, like, ever! "OK," Fern thought. "Let's get back to the Mehndi party before someone becomes suspicious."

On her way back, Fern tripped. She bashed against the wall.

"Ouch, that hurt," Fern muttered. "Actually, wait a second…"

She knocked on the wall with her knuckle.

Thud, thump, *thump*.

It was hollow! The wall was hollow!

She padded the wall, looking for a way to open it. There it was! It was a knob. She pushed it. There was a quiet creaking noise as the door panel slid open. Fern shook herself, ready for anything, and then walked in. She saw a staircase. She looked at it, wondering if it would hold, told herself not to worry and started climbing it.

At the top, there was a room. And, on the floor something glittered. What was that? There was something in front of it. It was a hedgehog! And not just any hedgehog. It was Honey, one of Dawn's friends! Thinking quickly, Fern grabbed her backpack and brought the camera out. She snapped a quiet picture. It was proof of the criminal. She would give it to the police and they could deal with Honey. That way she wouldn't have to do the scary stuff.

Quietly she went back down the staircase…

---

*A Mehndi party is the pre-wedding celebration in Hindu and Sikh culture, when the Bride has red-orange Mehndi 'stain or henna' applied to her palms, back of hands, and feet.

The Great Rainbow Trout Escape

By Wendy Ransom
Age 9

Wren was a happy rainbow trout, with a large and loving family. The only danger in his village was human fishnappers, but they never really bothered the town. Until one day when something terrible happened, something that shouldn't…

Wren woke with a yawn and bubbles rose up to the surface of the river and popped. He crawled out of his tiny crevice and swam up to Mum and Dad, who were looking concerned.

What's wrong?" asked Wren, but his question was answered by the thumping of feet and the shape of humans on the surface. The fishnappers were here.

"The bullfinch woke us up bright and early, calling about human activity," said Mum.

A great ball of anxiety, fear and curiosity overwhelmed him. Just then, 5 or so hooks tumbled into the water, each carrying some of the finest food Wren had ever seen. Wren knew the key to surviving was resisting the temptation of the food, but unfortunately (if you are a fish lover, I'd recommend skipping this part) Mum and Dad seemed to be too hungry.

"Oh dear," mumbled an old three-spined stickleback.

Wren wailed and tried to grab Mum's fin, though he slipped and she took a mouthful of the food. Suddenly there was a jerk as the rod went up, and Dad's was pulled too.

"Oh no!" said Wren as a strange feeling of pain and sadness washed over him like the river washed away silt

It slowly turned to anger, an urge for revenge and then the feel of an idea. He would leap into one of the tanks, smash the glass and save Mum and Dad. Simple. He slowly swum past the people, skilfully avoiding the hooks and swam to the tank. He leaped in and felt a feeling of airsickness. When he went up from the surface he saw something stranger than his wildest dream.

Tanks, 20 at least, were lined along the edge of the water. There were fish, tons of them, one species in each tank. There was even a bullfinch in a small box. The human who had been catching them had cinnamon hair and a red dress. She was clearly looking for something called a 'pet' (Mum had said that's an animal belonging to a human) as she had been saying "I will catch the perfect pet. I have to. I just must."

She clearly seemed pleased with her catch so far. She took Wren out and studied him. "He will look good with the rest of the rainbow trout," she said, and chucked Wren into the tank with his parents.

"Wren!" they cried.

"What are you doing here!?" asked Dad.

"I wanted to rescue you," said Wren, a little bit hurt that his parents hadn't realized what he was doing.

"That's nice, but how are we going to get out?" said Mum, quite worried by now.

Wren grinned. It was a big, broad smile. "Mum, Dad, when I say, hit the glass!"

They nodded.

"3… 2… 1… NOW!" he shouted.

They all hit the glass with their snouts (and the rest of their heads). Surprising force came out of this act and the glass smashed.

"What!?" said the humans, but it was too late! The rainbow trout had escaped to freedom.

Remember, there is not always another fish in the water. Never fish without an adult and permission from the landowner.

Shortlist

With so many incredible stories, it was almost impossible to choose just one! So here are the others that we loved as well.

The Twisted Meadow

By Tabby Bloomfield

I ran out of the house, slamming the door as I went. In my state of distress, I didn't notice the large crack in the path, causing me to trip and fall. I hit the ground hard and for a second the world seemed dark and warped.

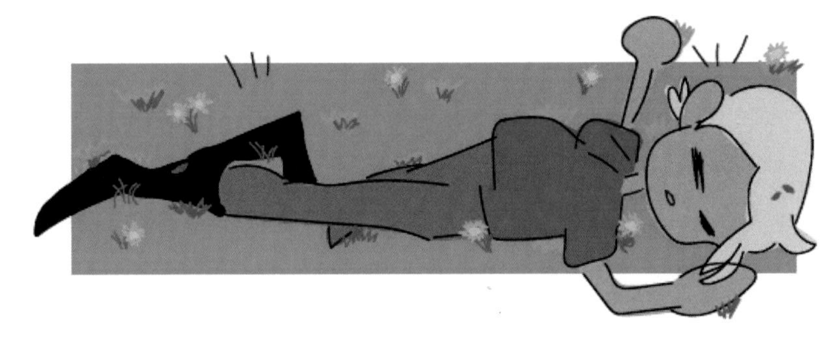

After a short amount of time, in which I cannot remember what happened, I stood up and was immediately captured by my surroundings. Somehow, I had woken up in a meadow that was teeming with life. There were ramsons, corncocks, columbines, kingcups and many other wildflowers that were too abstract to name. At a closer glance, hundreds of these flowers were holding bees who were going through with their busy lives.

All past feelings forgotten, I ran through this wondrous meadow, taking in all the natural beauty. The sound of cautious footsteps behind me snapped me out of my trance and I hastily spun on my heels, only to see a deer staring at me with slight curiosity, as if I was the first human to be here. I stepped forward, and to my surprise the deer stayed.

Something in my mind told me this place wasn't right. It was too perfect, but I ignored it. I was enjoying myself and paranoia wouldn't ruin that for me. I stayed there for who knows how long, dancing with the squirrels, bees, sparrows and flowers with a looming sense of danger at the back of my mind.

However, when the dark grey clouds rolled over the hills and all of the beauty vanished to be replaced by a gloomy sinister atmosphere, this sense became too strong to ignore. I stumbled, confused at how something so perfect could change into this.

As I glanced around, I realized that all the flowers had shrivelled and died and the only living creature left was the deer, which was staring at me with an odd look.

I gazed at it in confusion before realizing that the look was one of anger and hatred.

He was no longer curious about me. He had realised that I was trespassing on his territory.

I got closer, hoping to calm him, but stopped abruptly as I saw *it*. The reflection of something (or someone) in his eyes.

The thing smiled evilly as I saw it, and I ran. I ran from this non-perfect meadow. I didn't turn back and didn't stop until I was so tired I just collapsed, finally out of the glare of the deer.

Little did I know, I could never escape that deer, no matter how far I ran.

The Dragon-Mouse

By Dan Nixon

Ian was born in a field next to a zoo. Edinburgh Zoo to be exact, but that doesn't matter. What does matter, though, is that Ian thought that he was a dragon. It's a long story, but I've got 574 words, so I guess I'll tell you. When Ian was only a little mouse, about a week old, he scuttled under the zoo fence to explore.

He came out into the elephant enclosure, which was a huge coincidence, because he loved to listen to them hoot and trumpet in his burrow. Ian stood on his hind legs and said "Hello," as loud as he could. The elephant turned around and stared at him, and then… *HOOOOT!!!* The creature was terrified. It sounded like a whole brass band! The elephant ran into the corner and let out another, more quiet trumpeting noise.

Wow, Ian thought, *I must be terrifying if I could scare that thing. Maybe I'm not a mouse… What if I'm… A dragon!*

Ian stood on top of the zoo café roof. He had clambered up a pipe and he was going to try, at last, to fly. It had been 2 years since he had scared the elephant, and he was all grown up now. Yesterday, he had scared the lions, which further proved his slightly mad theory that he was a dragon. Ian had thought that since he was tiny.

All I have to do is jump.

Ian shivered. It was so high up. But what if he was one of those Chinese dragons that didn't have wings? What if he was too heavy for his wings to hold him up?

A caiman asked him, "What are you doing?"

Ian's simple answer came; "I'm going to fly."

"Err, no you aren't, you're a mouse."

"No, I'm not," Ian said sternly, "I'm a dragon, and I'll prove it."

He spread his arms out theatrically, and then jumped. Flapping his arms uselessly, he fell for what seemed like an eternity. The caiman leaped forward, and caught Ian in his claws.

"See?" the caiman said. "You can't fly. You're a mouse."

Maybe I'm not a dragon, Ian thought. *Maybe I am just a mouse.*

The next day, Ian was trying to breathe fire.

He stood in front of an empty container and focused on his breathing.

An ostrich behind the nearby fence said, "Boy is it cold… I wish I had maybe a fire, or a heater… Or a dragon to breath fire!"

Ian stared at the ostrich and explained bumptiously, "Well, now's your lucky day! As a matter of fact, I am a dragon. I was just about to set fire to this container, so maybe you could bring it over the fence to keep you warm!"

The ostrich stared in confusion.

"Well, first of all, it's plastic and not flammable. Second of all, you cannot breathe fire, you're a mouse." The ostrich said this quite snootily, then she paused and thought about her next point. "And third of all a tiny fire isn't going to keep me warm, I'm too big of an animal."

Ian just shot a look at the ostrich and opened his mouth. Breathing out forcefully, he tried and tried, even taking another breath, but still, he couldn't even make a spark.

"Listen little guy," said the ostrich, "you aren't a dragon. You're a mouse. I'm sorry."

Ian sighed. "Maybe I am…"

"At least mice are cool," said the ostrich.

Enchanted Forest

By Maja Kudzma

In the heart of the canopy of lofty trees, there lay a frosty blue eyed girl glaring at the miraculous enchanted forest. Her name was Maya. She lived there, in a small cottage with her beastly aunt Bertha. Maya absolutely hated her, she was so repulsive with her pongy and earsplitting voice but worse, she hated animals!!! Spacious animals, pitch black jaguars even. For short she hated all animals.

Maya strolled inside the cottage.

Suddenly Bertha bellowed, "Get inside and do the dishes you stupid animal!" She snarled and idly grabbed a pack of mouldy, old chips. Maya frantically ran inside and saw her aunty eating those greasy, repugnant again. Her eyes turned rusty red seeing it. "Hurry up," aunty Bertha cursed. Maya ignored her and wanted escape from her violent aunty. How could she do that? She watched her aunty scratch her armpits and darted straight into her bedroom.

Maya thought about the terrific forest and the amazing beauty of it. Maya just couldn't take her aunty anymore and hefted herself. She rapidly scampered away, so she was so far in the forest. She jolted over gnarled, wrinkled tree roots and looked upon the magnificent forest.

She could see a vile looking, jaw breakingly, razor sharp mountain. Some fern like plants were wrapped around her ankles. Thin slivers of sunlight shone through towering lofty trees. There was an azure cascading waterfall in the distance. Maya quickened her pace. It was the brink of dusk. A mist submerged the whole forest.

"Arrrrgh," Maya bellowed. Glorious, green plants turned to a smoky grey. Owls shrieked. Maya lay paralyzed with horror.

Meanwhile in a vast clearing, there was a crazy scientist guy named Fujimayoto. He came from deepest, darkest sandiest Mongolian desert. He had wacky, bushy eyebrows and sly eyes and a peculiar smirk. He looked always sinister! He wore exquisite uniform. Fujimayoto had melancholic life. He wanted revenge. His plan was to burn half of the forest so he could build his gem factory.

Back in the forest depths. Maya scurried inside a cave. After that, she sat bolt upright. Suddenly the floor disappeared.

"Aaaa," Maya screeched abruptly. She thought she was going to perish.

The sky turned pitch black. A fountain of flames engulfed the whole forest! There was an eerie deafening sound.

The crazy, mad scientist was covered with soot and sweat, his hands were also oozing with tar. He had a violent, breath-taking voice. Blood vibrated through her hands and feet. The scientist took out the extremely dangerous weapon and grunted, "What are you doing here nitwit?!!!!!"

Bile swelled up in Maya's throat. Fujimayoto pointed a gun at her. As quick as a flash a group of animals scampered in. Maya was next to agile swift squirrel. It stared at her with emerald, green eyes. It looked like it was very intelligent and cunning. Its fur was gingery orange. There was another animal with silk fur, gloomy eyes. It looked bewildered. He was transporting a putrid apple.

"Let's do this," stuttered the animal vulnerably. Some more animals appeared.

The scientist launched squirrel in the air but the smart creature landed on its paws.

"Now!!!" screeched the animal. A second later all the animals charged at the crazy scientist, but he took out his machine gun. The creatures didn't stop and tug on his clothes and ripped them. Maya grasped all his weapons and called the police. The scientist was defeated!!!

Food Thief

By Lucy Ribchester
Age 9

As the sun crept into a deep sleep and the moon did its nightly routine, a small dog-like animal with pointed ears, glistening eyes and soft, orange fur trotted unknown into an overgrown, muddy clearing.

"I-it's s-s-so c-c-cold a-and w-w-wet!" Freya the Fox muttered under her breath. As she wandered deeper into the clearing Freya thought more and more about how she longed to get the food quickly so she could get back to her warm, cosy den with her adorable children. While her paws immediately set to work scraping away the soil and her nose tried to pick up any scent of worms, Freya's brain eagerly thought of ideas of how to get the rest of her body up and going home. A long time after she arrived, Freya had dug deep underground without finding a single, tiny, worm to eat! Eventually she just gave up and went to search the bushes for fruit – no berries there either! After searching every nook and cranny of every bush, she just gave up and went home without dinner! Later that cold, rainy night the headline on her newspaper was:

FOOD THIEF

Under the title it said:

Has your food gone missing?

We know who took the food: The Food Thief!

It also said

Whoever catches the mysterious Food Thief

will get the feast of food that the Food Thief stole.

"That is the job for me! Oooh, and a feast reward! I am definitely going to catch that thief!" she whisper-shouted excitedly.

Freya made a plan. She thought that she would rent a private jet and fly all over Animal Island in search of any hidden hideout or maybe a hideout easily seen but really hard to get into.

She would use her karate skills and the sharpest knives that she had to cut vines or stop booby traps! She would also bring rope to tie around the Food

Thief when she jumped out from where she was hiding in the Food Thief's hideout.

After she did all of the paperwork and learnt to fly a jet, she got into a beautiful gold plane with silver wings and shiny windows and started the engine dramatically.

Freya soared into the calm, fresh air and did an impressive back flip (scaring all of the birds)! She swooped through all of the trees and danced on mountains (with the plane of course!). As she came in to do the best loop the loop that the world had ever seen, she noticed something and stopped concentrating on the flying so

BOOM!

SMACK!

CRASH!

Freya almost fainted! She had crashed into a huge, old, wrinkly oak tree. But Freya didn't care because she had seen something unusual! There was a green flag fluttering in the wind almost camouflaged by the tall endless trees. She rubbed her bruises and scampered over to the flag. It was rusty but it was shiny and it had trees and flowers decorated around it. Freya leaned closer.

"AAAArrrrgghh!! Make it stoooop!!" she screamed wildly. Freya had stepped on a trap door! She had fallen on to a pile of crusty leaves covered in thick mud layered in pinecones. "Ouch!" she screamed uncontrollably. Freya got up and dusted herself down. She stared around; mouth open. On a sign right in front of her a message was printed.

It said:

Benny Badger AKA The Food Thief

"I need to hide quickly," Freya gasped. "This is the Food Thief's hideout."

Freya leaped behind piles and piles of dirty dishes filled with old food just as another animal fell through the trap door. But he didn't look surprised to have fallen and actually he turned out to be a badger!

"That must be him," she thought without a doubt. She grabbed her rope enthusiastically and threw it at the badger with such force that it knocked him down! Freya ran to him and tied him up with her thick, unbreakable rope. She then grabbed the old-fashioned, dusty phone from the wall and dialled 999. It turned out that the police had been looking for this thief for 21 years because he had committed several other robberies, including stealing valuable objects that were worth millions of pounds!

So the police got there extra quickly to see if Freya had actually captured the Food Thief and indeed she had. So, as said in the newspaper, she got the humongous feast of food that Benny had stolen. As predicted, the day after Freya succeeded in capturing the thief, she had a huge feast with her family. You could smell delicious smells coming from the kitchen and you could hear the kettle boiling. It really was a great day.

The End

Animals Life

By Ted Winship

Hi, I am Bob!

I live in tiny town. We have cars made out of wood and planes made out of leaves but my favourite are the houses. They are mushrooms, get it mush-rooms.

Anyway, this town sounds like the best place on earth, but all stories have a twist, ours is the humans. We have no food, so we have to steal lots and lots of food to hibernate. But we have to be careful which my parents weren't. They rushed into the human town, the last part of them was mum's necklaces.

Now I live with my grandma, she is a bit bonkers, but she is fine for someone who looks after me.

This story began when the humans were our friends. They fed us, they looked after us, they slept with us. Until a new king rose, he hated animals and told the humans to attack all of the animals. Of course they obeyed him, we had to scram into the woods and make a new life. If one of the humans didn't do what the king said they would be cursed forever. Which has happened before to a guy called Freddy. Now our aim is to take out the king and bring happiness to the land. When it's an animal's birthday we celebrate by stealing 500 pieces of food for the family. The humans celebrate by sobbing around all day, no offence if you are a human.

Mostly humans eat cake, sweets, salad and pizza, all we have now is wood that's why we steal. Human classrooms are so sophisticated, all we have is a stone and a leaf to write on.

We don't even get phones, we only have wood. Some of the humans don't really care and drop plastic on the ground which can kill us. It can be so bad some of us will have to go to hospital.

So please don't litter and save us and Tiny town!

The Runaway Rabbit

By Oliver Wilson
Age 11

Shearer is a house rabbit who lives with me, Oliver, but he has a story to tell about his escape from home. Enjoy!

Shearer the house rabbit began to scratch at his bedroom door with his paws. Eventually Oliver, his human, got up to feed him (it was 6am).

Shearer was having a great day. He chased the dog, Skye, up and down the stairs, he sunbathed on the windowsill and he was jumping up on the sofa and just having the best time. His great day was going so well until Oliver and his Mother decided to go to Rainton Meadows (part of the Durham Wildlife Trust). They lived just a field away from Rainton meadows. Shearer was so disappointed that he had to be locked in his room whilst they were away that he made a plan. A plan to escape the house…

Shearer was an intelligent bunny. He knew that there was a window open a little in the kitchen so he jumped up and got through it and jumped down onto the lawn. He hopped to the back of the garden where there was a perfect grass patch to begin digging. He dug and dug and dug until he ended up outside his garden and then he quickly followed his nose to what he hoped would be a great adventure and it was… to Rainton Meadows Coffee Shop!

Shearer snuck out past the coffee shop and ended up at Joe's Pond. In the distance he could see more rabbits so he hopped over to go and say 'hello'. The rabbits greeted him and welcomed him. Shearer was free and was now a wild rabbit… or was he?

The rabbits had so much fun together. They dug holes, they chased ducks and were having the best time ever.

The other wild bunnies loved swimming but Shearer wasn't so sure as he was quite chubby for a rabbit and probably wouldn't float, but in a shallow bit of water he practiced and ended up getting quite good. He beat all of the rabbits in a swimming race and became the best of them all!

Meanwhile… After visiting the gift shop and the coffee shop, Oliver and his mum decided to go for a walk round Joe's Pond. Oliver saw some wild rabbits and he loved rabbits so he slowly edged closer to see more clearly.

Oliver could see a black and white rabbit.

Hmm, he thought, *that looks like Shearer's twin!*

Rainton Meadows really is a beautiful place to be, thought Shearer, and then he saw Oliver and Oliver's mum. Just then a fox came round and all the rabbits scattered and Shearer ran towards his human, Oliver, for protection.

"Mum," said Oliver. "It really is Shearer."

"It can't be," said Oliver's Mum, but yes it definitely was.

Shearer ran into Oliver's outstretched arms and snuggled his face next to Oliver's.

"Well," said Shearer to himself. "Rainton Meadows and all the animals are beautiful, and I've enjoyed my adventure today, but I've always been a house rabbit and I suppose I always will be."

Oliver promised to take Shearer to visit Rainton Meadows when he could – and he has kept that promise… But Shearer always keeps an eye out for foxes.

"Remember," says Shearer, "All animals, wild or domestic, deserve to be loved and cared for and not harmed or exploited."

The Wishing River

By Gwen Uckelman
Age 9

Once, a long time ago, there was a barred grass snake called Trevor, and he lived in a river in Niji called Elphant. It was called this because it was shaped like an Elephant. People rarely visited this part of Niji because there was a ferocious water dragon named Terror who roamed the river. No-one dared to venture down to see him. Not even brave Trevor dared. But one day he wished *he* could be a dragon. But the only way he could was if he went over Frostmount to get to the Wishing River. So he decided to set out on his journey to that special river tomorrow bright and early (even though he was not a morning snake).

When he woke up it was already 8:30am and he was late to get going. He slipped out of his pajamas and packed his suitcase until it was full to the brim. He put his hat on and slithered out of the water onto the path. There standing right in front of him was Frostmount with its towering peaks that struck the sky. He did not want to leave his wet and cosy home in Elphant. But he had to, to get to the Wishing River.

He was halfway up the mountain when the sun sank behind the trees. When he woke the next morning he noticed that he had forgotten his watch and didn't know what time it was, so he set off. Trevor didn't know that it was only 6:45am so when he got to the other side of the mountain it was almost 11:40 and his tummy was grumbling. It wasn't just because he was hungry, but also because there was a strong smell of frogs with mushy worms (Trevor's usual breakfast) coming from a small cottage.

He went up to the door and took the knocker, but hesitated before knocking. There was a long silence before the door opened, and out stepped a grey heron(Trevor had been wondering why the door was so tall).

"I haven't had a visitor in such a long time!" exclaimed the heron, surprised and excited at the thought. "The name's Henry, what's yours?"

"I'm Trevor," said Tevor.

"Would you like to join me for some lunch?"

"Yes, please," Trevor said hungrily. He sat down at a small table and Henry put a big plate of food in front of him. The snake dug into his meal and was soon having his second helping. After his third helping he remembered why he came.

"I'll see you later, I have to run, bye!"

Trevor dashed out of the door and all the way to the Wishing River. He was running so fast that he ended up speeding right into the river with a splash. It felt nice after all those days out of the water. Then he remembered the thing he had to say:

"I wish I could be a dragon."

He felt his wriggly body growing fins and his tail and neck getting longer and longer. He swam in circles of joy. He burst out of the water and yelled "hey Henry, I did it! *I'm a water dragon*!"

Henry rushed out of his house with a grin on his face and gave him a big, wet hug.

"Now I have to go, but I will come and visit you as often as I can!"

The End

The Mystery

By Millie He
Aged 9

As the fox drove his taxi, he noticed a hedgehog standing in the cold rain. So he decided to give her a free lift to where she wanted to go. The fox opened the door and walked slowly to the hedgehog.

"Hi, I'm sorry to bother you but do you need a lift? It's for free I promise," said the Fox. The hedgehog just gave him a note saying "Yes".

"Okay then, follow on," said the Fox. "So, where can I take you ma'am?" questioned the Fox curiously. The hedgehog passed a note saying, "to the graveyard please".

The Fox thought *"B-but there's only one graveyard here a-and it's abandoned!"* He started to get goosebumps but said, "Sure!"

He started driving but then he looked behind him and the hedgehog was mysteriously gone, blood was on the seat. The Fox got really scared and stopped the taxi to look properly and this time she was there holding a note saying "I'm coming."

The Fox grabbed it and ripped it. He started driving again and he realised that she was asleep and she had the same note again. As soon as they reached the stop the door opened without her touching it. She entered and disappeared. He drove home and drank his soup slowly. He looked at the TV and it was the same hedgehog that he saw.

The Badger said, "we found a dead body near the abandoned graveyard." He was shocked and could hear an animal scratching his door. He decided to open it shivering with fear and saw scratches but nobody there.

Special Mentions

Although the following stories didn't win, they still ooze with whimsy and charm.

Gracie the Great

By Esmae Thompson

In a tree far far away…

There lived a magical owl named Gracie, she lived with her sister Rosie. They were about to go on an extremely important mission to save their long lost mum and dad (who were trapped in an abandoned forest in the country: Prance. They have been trapped there since 1999 by an evil crow called Shadow.

So at 12:00pm midnight Gracie and Rosie set off on their journey to Prance. The flew like the wind over lots of countries: Englandia, Busha, Bafrica and even Zongolia.

After the whole night had past, children started to wake up in their houses and peer out of the window to spot two flying creatures…Oh no! They were being spotted everywhere. There were pictures on billboards and TVs. They stayed lots of nights in different forests all over the world and made lots of friends who told them about the evil crow.

The next day, they reached Prance and found the abandoned forest but didn't know what to do because it was an amber list country. They came across lots of friendly animals such as: bunnies, worms and lots of birds but surprisingly no one was as nice as the evil crow (who wasn't actually so evil after all).

He made them a garland made from daisies to welcome them to Prance, the forest was not actually abandoned either it was very pretty with lots of wildlife growing. They asked if he knew where their parents were… He burst out into happy tears, he said that they'd been worrying about Gracie and Rosie ever since they got lost there.

Suddenly there was a noise. "Twiiiittt awooooo," says the darkness, and again "twiiittt awooooo". And there were their parents, spilling out of the tree to greet them with a big warm hug. After a while of crying, they all decided to live in the not so abandoned forest with the not so evil crow.

The Journey

By Ellie Doughty, Age 9

I am Bindi and I am a Fox.

I live in a Fox mansion. I have a friend who is called Lulu and she is a Hedgehog. Lulu lives with me and my other friend is called Moonlight. She lives next door to me and she is an Owl. She lives in a owl mansion with her dad. Moonlight's mum died when she was little. Lulu's mum and dad died in an attack in their house.

I just live on my own. I woke up to see that Lulu was in my bedroom. My dad says that my mum died. But I don't believe that my mum is dead. I wanted to prove that mum was still alive. So I set off on a Journey. I asked my friends if they would come with me. Lulu said yes and Moonlight said yes.

So the Journey begins. But Moonlight's dad stopped us because he didn't want to lose her. Moonlight's dad said "you're not going anywhere so you're staying with me."

Moonlight had to sneak away from dad when he was asleep. Moonlight snuck out and said that her dad was asleep. Moonlight left a letter saying where she is going and who she is with. I said to my dad that I was going on a journey and I said don't worry I'll be safe. So we set off on our journey to see if my mum is still alive. We had to go through the lake to camp. It was the morning and they were all up. We went past lots of animals. I saw my mum's best friends and she said that she is still alive. But although she might be alive she might have died. My mum was called Piper and my dad is called Max. I woke up in a deep dark cave and there were only trees surrounding me. I saw a tail and it was not Lulu or Moonlight. So it was something else. I thought to myself it was a Fox or Badger. I said, "who is it?' I am a Fox and what is your name? My name is Bindy. What is your name," I said.

"My name is Piper," the Fox said.

I said, "Is that you mum?"

"Is that you Bindi?" asked Piper. "Yes it is."

"Mum, where are you?"

"I'm here."

"Can I take you home mum?"

"No, because it is dangerous."

"Please mum."

Me and mum set off to animal city. We arrived home but dad was not there. He left a letter saying that someone is looking for you and mum. It said I am hurt and I've gone to kill however I want. I want to go and find my dad. When I find him I am going to kill the beast but there is a war going on so I have to find my dad first. I was a bit scared but I was able to find my dad. We arrived at the beast hideout. My dad said it was a female and she was laying eggs.

So me and my dad went home but suddenly we saw a male. We knew that one was after me and mum. We had to kill the male, so we did. We went back home. Dad was so happy that mum was back.

Flavia's Hamburger Disaster

By Sally Stephenson

As Flavia the fox cautiously stepped out of her burrow in the wood, under the great oak tree, she found herself surrounded by trees. She was hungry and so were her mum, dad and brothers. When she got near to the edge of the town, a gorgeous smell wafted up her wet, black nose. She knew that smell anywhere. Hamburgers, juicy, yummy hamburgers! She knew that they would be perfect for the family of five. She set off in search of the smell.

The smell grew stronger and stronger as she weaved through the dirty scrap yards and over dustbins, going through noisy streets until she saw tall, fleshy things. Dangerous, fleshy things. After what felt like a year, Flavia saw a huge sign saying, in flickering letters, 'Burger lovers come here'. She slipped silently round the back way and found that to her disappointment the doors were jammed shut tightly!

Suddenly, a cute little squirrel hopped out of the bushes, nibbling a blackberry. She squeaked,

"There was a thunder storm and now the doors won't work. There is still one way you can get in though."

"How?" Flavia demanded.

"You learn karate." she squeaked, like it was a normal thing to say.

"I learn what?" Flavia said, shocked!

"Karate," she said. "My name is Nibbles and if you want to get in, you'll need to learn karate!"

Suddenly a loud CRACK, BOOM, CRASH filled the air! The thunderstorm had returned.

"Quick follow me if you want burgers!" said Nibbles.

They darted down an open manhole cover that was nearby where to Flavia's great surprise there where three other squirrels dressed in white lacy clothes.

"This is Bobby, Nobby and Crobby." Nibbles squeaked.

Looking around, Flavia realised that Nibbles was now wearing similar clothes too. One of the squirrels dashed off and a couple of minutes later he gave her a set of Karate Gi too.

Within one hour Flavia had learned all the basic karate moves and they where ready to rumble. Their soft bodies crept out and they went to the door of the hamburger shop. Without hesitating, Flavia pulled out the best move ever and...

SMASH!

CRASH!

TINKLE!

...the glass shattered. Nobby squeezed inside and pulled out not one, not two, not three, not four, not five, not six, not seven, not eight, but nine hamburgers, one for each of the squirrels, Flavia and her family. They all went to back to Flavia's den and tucked into the hamburgers. Maybe, just maybe, we'll have steak tomorrow, Flavia wondered!

The Blood Moon

By Samuel Stokes, aged 9

After raiding nearly all the bins of Bowling Square, Freddie the Fox trotted back into the haunted woods carrying his loot. As he walked through the haunted woods, Freddie wondered to himself when the Blood Moon would be coming. He knew that this year it would be delayed but he didn't know how long it would be delayed for. When he got to his burrow he looked around to see no one was watching him and knocked. No answer. Again, he knocked. But this time a slit opened in the ground by his feet and a rough voice called out, 'What's the password mate?'.

Freddie replied with 'Red Wood'. There was a creaking noise, like the opening of a chest which had not been opened for a century, and slowly the burrow door opened.

The burrow market was echoing with the noise of a hundred foxes. As Freddie walked past carrying his loot, the lights turned off and the sirens sounded for a blood moon. At once all of the foxes rushed through the many doorways in the walls of the burrow to their rooms. A few trapdoors in the ceiling opened and part of the fox army jumped out. One of the leaders from the fox army ran to the entrance and pressed a big red button. As soon as he had pressed the big red button, the entrance to the market slammed shut and the lights turned on. But this time they were a blood red colour – exactly the colour of the blood moon.

In Freddie's burrow, and most of the other burrows, all hell was breaking loose. There were foxes slamming shut their windows and blocking their doors with any material they could find. And each of the trapdoors in every burrow ceiling had already dropped out weapons for the foxes inside. And in Freddie's burrow these weapons were two maces, three swords and a shield for each of them. And in Freddie's ginormous burrow, two bodyguards came charging through the door for the five foxes aka Freddie, Fiona, Faraaz, Charles and Greta. Outside, the fox army were at their positions putting up watchtowers as it was nearly night. In the tree which was on top of the fox burrow, the red squirrels, who are the foxes' friends were getting their acorn missile catapults ready for the oncoming attacks of badgers.

As the sirens predicted, it was a blood moon tonight. But surprisingly, the fox guard were waiting for over an hour before the Badger waves came. When the Badger waves came, like the many times before, they started off easy and as they carried on they got harder. At around 1am in the morning a wave of Badgers came and this time they broke through the defences and then broke down the burrow door. The Fox guards inside were highly trained but they had never been trained for soldiers as well-equipped and skilled as these badgers. It was a tough battle in the burrow market place but more badger waves came into support the badgers already there and the fox soldiers were defeated.

The badgers broke into all the rooms in the burrow and raided them. But as they broke into Freddie's burrow, the booby traps which Freddie had set caught out about 20 of the 100 badgers that came in. So Freddie, his bodyguards and his family were able to take out the rest, that was the last wave of badgers for the night. The surviving foxes crept out of the burrow to check what time it was. It was early morning. The red squirrels who had been on top of the tree scrambled down to meet the surviving foxes. A few of the red squirrels had been taken out by the badgers with ranged weapons but there were still quite a few red squirrels remaining. Together they managed to rebuild the burrow. And after a week the burrow was completely rebuilt and as good as new. And they added in more security alarms and booby traps.

And they all lived happily ever after, until the next blood moon came and most of them died. But then they rebuilt the burrow and this carried on for the next few centuries until they found a way to stop the blood moon forever.

The End

Independence

By Harrison Miller, Aged 9

As the sun started its descent and the birds quietened their evening's song, Rex the fox trotted purposefully through the sleeping woods in search of some supper. It was getting darker now but Rex still trotted onwards. Just then he felt a drop of water on his nose and the growl of thunder in the distance. He realised that there was a storm brewing. Rex had heard thunder before and didn't like it. He was scared.

Rex decided to run back to his den. Just as he was approaching the entrance, the big oak tree above the den was struck by lightning and crashed to the ground, completely destroying the den. His heart sank. Everything he had ever known was gone.

He needed to find food and his family. He decided that the best thing to do was to start his search now. The storm was very close. He could hear the thunder roaring and the lightning forks were crashing through the canopy, lighting up the night sky.

The next day, after sleeping at his friend's burrow, Rex set off on his search. Many moons passed and he still could not find anything. He had only eaten a salmon and he was very hungry.

Suddenly there was a rustle in the bushes and out came a family of rabbits, plump, furry rabbits. A thought came into his head. At last he could eat, could have a feast all to himself. The chase was on. They started sprinting through the woods but Rex was weak as he hadn't eaten for days. However, the rabbits did not escape. The strength of the fox's hunger was too much for the rabbits and their young lives were taken away. They were supper.

After Rex's scrumptious dinner, he carried on. Later that evening he came to a clearing and he saw a crack in the earth. He approached cautiously and stared down. There was lava. Hot, bubbling lava.

"Hello," said a voice to the right of him. Startled, he jumped round. It was a grass snake who was guarding a bridge to the other side of the crack.

"Going somewhere punk?" asked the grass snake. Rex plucked up courage to fight the snake. The battle commenced. They started ramming into each other and scuffling around on the ground. The snake had Rex pinned down over the crack. He sighed in disappointment. Just then, Rex though of a way to beat the snake. He lashed out his bushy tail and struck the reptile down, down into the lava. He could hear the loud screams of agony as they echoed through the crack as the lava burned flesh from its body.

Rex did feel sorry for the snake, but he had no choice but to do it. He crossed the bridge and trotted on into the woods. As the morning started a new day he went deeper into the woods. Just at that moment, he heard a bark. It was a fox's bark. He recognised it immediately. He was sure it was his mother's bark. He barked back in reply and started running through bushes and round trees. He had finally found his parents or at least one. When they found each other, Rex asked his mum where his dad was. Her face fell and with a tremble in her voice she told Rex what had happened. The deadly storm had killed his dad. Rex told his mum what had happened to him. Together they decided to build a new den.

Three fox years passed and mother and son continued to live happily in their comfortable home.

The Adventure of Lottie and Max

By Iris Foulger, Aged 9

Early one morning Lottie Johnson woke up and she checked her watch. It said 06:30. So she crept downstairs and got a piece of paper and a pencil. Then she quietly went back upstairs and tried to decide what to draw. Lottie liked drawing animals and her dream pet would be a fox, so she drew a picture of a fox and called it Max.

When she was finished the time was 07:08. She got dressed and went downstairs to have breakfast. Her mum was already downstairs, making toast.

After school, Lottie went back to her house to pick up her mum so they could go on their afternoon walk through the forest. At school everyone had got told that they had to do a short story about British Wildlife. Everyone was super excited and couldn't wait to do it.

When Lottie got home from school the next day she found out that her mum wasn't there. She thought that her mum was just at the shop so she went on the walk herself and she found out a fox had started following her. So she kept it and named it Max.

When she got back her house was destroyed and Max had saw hunters running away. Then Max took Lottie to his home but some foxes were gone. Both Lottie and Max tried to track down the hunters and find Lottie's mum and the rest of the foxes, but they couldn't get through because lots of different animals were blocking their path. While Max was distracting them, Lottie ran straight past and into the hunters home. Inside what looked like a mansion were lots of swords and daggers that what Lottie thought were for hunting animals.

Max saved the day when they met up with the hunters because he ran out of the mansion and the hunters ran after him because the fox is all they had wanted. Then Lottie ran through every room, but eventually she stopped because she saw something amazing or in Lottie's case cruel. On each wall in the room were animals heads hanging on the wall and one was even a fox head. She muttered to herself "I need to get rid of these hunters!" Then she looked in each cell and eventually found her mum and all of the foxes that had all been lost, but her mum was badly hurt!

Lottie took her to hospital and then Max was able to get rid of the hunters and came back to Lottie. In the end Lottie and her mum were able to live on a farm for very little money and they were allowed to keep all the animals, but Lottie's favourite was always Max. (Though she did like her hedgehog as well.)

The Seed Planters

By Joe Foulger, Aged 9

Long ago, a house set deep in the heart of a forest started to creak in the sky, it was time for the foxes to come out. Now, like most readers I bet that you probably are very fussy and you might be saying to yourself something like "Foxes, that is just sooooooo boring, I'm gonna go get a more interesting book, like The Big Book Of Excitement," but guess what? Read on and you will be intrigued.

The seed planters are foxes that came out every night to plant poppy seeds in their home of soil. Next to the forest was a field, the field of war the animals called it. It was true, there was constant fighting again and again and worst of all the factory making the weapons damaged their home!

One day there was a huge fire, the factory had made a new weapon, the bomb!

The fire spread everywhere, demolishing everything in the forest, the only things that were safe were the animals. The seed planters helped everyone to get to safety and then they began their long journey to find another home, but the question was who was the owner of the weapons company called Acompany? Nobody knows, but the seed planters want to find out.

When they travelled along the muddy field, the bag containing the poppy seeds got caught on a branch. As the foxes and other animals were still walking, the bag toppled to the ground and as it did so the wind picked them up and they scattered along the muddy field. None stuck together and soon the field was full of seeds in every place, and ever so slowly they started to grow. When the animals found a camp they vowed towards the humans to get revenge on them.

Early the next morning, all the animals got up and travelled to Acompany to stop it working completely. As they walked, they stumbled across a group of wolves. The wolves were running straight towards them, all of them were frightened of something, something more frightening than every lion put together. It was fire. The fire spread faster and faster towards them all and as suddenly as they appeared they stopped, paused, and kept on running, this time more franticly than before.

When they finally reached us they just kept on going, they jumped into a lake, they took their bags, emptied everything out and tipped all their water on the fire, that put it out and then then proceeded on their journey. As they came across Acompany, they realised they did not need to destroy the factory, they needed to stop the war. They changed direction and headed for the battlefield. When they got there they thought of turning back, for the battlefield was murky and dirty, the battle was horrifying to watch but they knew that they couldn't turn back. So they got a metal box full of blanks, they then stood on lots of them and made as much noise as they could. It just was not loud enough, then out of the corner of their eyes they saw a shop, a radio shop. The foxes with their agile legs leapt, took a recorder from the shop, and turned it on and explained everything that had happened. Everybody stopped fighting and listened and it all stopped.

With me I think that the poppy seeds made this happen, they may be lucky.

Bongo's Beans

By Leo Pippet, Aged 9

Hi! I am bongo the badger. I steal food from everywhere, so let's have a look at my story.

One day I was stealing food, when I saw some magic beans and stole them too.

Then I got home the beans glowed vibrant green!!! There was a label on the back that said

Please put me
On the highest tree
For I will make money for thee!!!

On my way to the tree, I ran and ran for miles until I was cold because I had reached the shadow of the highest tree.

Suddenly I was attacked by Foxy Loxy and Sammy the SNAKE!! So I boomed a huge squawk and all of the bird army attacked and defeated Sammy and Foxy. Then Gruffy the Golden eagle swooped down. The leader bird also swooped down and fought Gruffy until he was blasted into the sky and never returned!!!

I managed to get up the tree and plant the beans. The beans turn into a potion that makes them into crystallised money. After that I go and play with Brothy the raven so we make diamond charms.

The End

The Zombie Apocalypse

By Louis Dresser, Aged 9

In the heart of a forest Bill the squirrel is having tea by himself. Outside he sees a zombie turning all the animals into zombies. He quickly runs outside seeing a piece of paper that says if you find this crystal in a cave and destroy it the zombies will turn back into animals. Bill goes on a hunt to get the crystal and destroy it.

Bill goes to find the crystal. As he starts the quest, he sees some zombies coming after him! Bill runs away from them and into a mysterious building. He looks inside the building and sees a bunch of zombies! Bill sees a trapdoor, so he quickly goes inside.

Once inside the trapdoor he sees the crystal and grabs it and throws it on the floor, but it doesn't break! He tries again but it still doesn't break. Then he sees a note that says to break the crystal you will need a hammer, so Bill goes to the DIY store, but they have ran out of hammers!

So, he goes to another DIY store and finds a hammer and it breaks the crystal and all the zombies turn back into animals. Except the zombie that started the apocalypse - he disintegrated into dust! All the animals cheer for Bill and say how can we repay you?

So, Bill ends up getting the world's biggest tree to live in, it has 20 bedrooms, 5 kitchens, 10 living rooms and a lot more rooms so Bill ends up living happily ever after.

The End

Finding Home

By Maria Welsh, Aged 9

When I was just a little lamb, our farm was a dream.

Now I'm a bit older and it has completely changed. Not only I'm one of the only sheep, we had to move in with the cows. Now all we do is argue with the cows about who's home it is.

Recently, I overheard the farmer say that we didn't have enough money and we will be sent to a meat shop! Now I am running to the front of the line so I can be sheared first.

Phew I'm done, I can get on with my journey.

I need to find a new home. "Hello anyone here?" I ask just stumbling through the forest entrance. The only sound I hear back is the squawking and crowing of the birds. The squirrels scamper down the trees while the owls sleep in their trees. I see a ball in the tree and a badger in its sett I better move.

The forest behind my farm is very big also might have to search for a few days. But today it's Saturday and we will be taken on Monday. I'm tripping and stumbling on the hollow tree roots. The sound of my friends in the distance. The hawk spots me and I am running for my life. My mum said to watch out for badgers I have already seen one.

"Hey squirrel can you help me. What's your name." I'm asking trying to find someone who knows the woods.

"Sam and what's your name?"

"Sheep don't have names apart from nine or something. Oh well, I'm looking for a new home. And I'm a girl by the way."

"I'm looking for a new home too."

"Let's team up." We're off to find a new home now and the trees are even bumper.

"I think we might have to make a shelter. It's getting late." I say. We build the shelter so that hawks and badgers can't get in.

Hungry Animals

By Lucas Manzi, Aged 9

Down in the depths of the quite nice farm, there lived PIGSTER the leader, not the average pig you would find on a farm. So meet Squirrel aka the nonstop bottle of fizz pop on the team, the energy you might say. Finally there's COW, the brains of the team. Today it's a normal day for the team.

"What are you doing today?" asks Pigster

"Usual thing, eating grass. What are you doing today?" asked Cow.

"Same as you, eating grass." said Pigster. That is how boring the animals life was.

Until the farmer ran out of food and went MAD! He was going to cook pig!

"I've got a question?" asked Pigster.

"What is your question?" said Cow

"Aren't farmers meant to look after their animals?"

"WHO WANTS SAUSAGES!" shouted the farmer.

"RUN!" shouted Pigster. Then Pigster, Cow and Squirrel raced over their fences and ran for their lives.

They ran for miles before they started to get hungry. Luckily there were lots of food stands but you had to pay three pounds for each snack and the shopkeepers weren't so forgiving. The animals just ran through the food stands chomping on foods that they normally eat. But one of the farmers caught Squirrel but neither of them noticed he was gone. Pigster and Cow got past the next ten food stands until Cow noticed Squirrel was gone and called Pigster. He noticed and fainted.

Pigster woke up and Cow was watching him eye to eye, "Mother of little piggies, what in sausages name were you watching me like that for!" shouted Pigster.

"I was waiting until you woke up so we could go rescue Squirrel," said Cow.

"Well never do that again then!"

Meanwhile, Squirrel was trapped in a corner with the crazed shopkeeper watching him.

"So Squirrel you vant your friends back do you," began the shopkeeper, "Vell guess vat they are not coming back!" said the shopkeeper

"Oh yes we are!" bellowed Pigster and pounded the crazed shopkeeper with his own fruit watermelon, melon, blueberries.

"I knew I shouldn't have sold fruits!" cried the shopkeeper.

While Pigster was doing that Cow unlocked Squirrel and they all left.

All of the team had forgotten the pig, sausage incident and raced back to the farm.

In the end the farmer had heaps of food and there were decorations everywhere. Could the farmer be hosting a party...?

Booming Badger

By Mason Smith, Aged 9

There was a booming badger called Killer.

He was in the wild woods, he was sneakily crawling in the woods and saw a lumberjack.

Booming badger stuck his sharp bleeding claws into the lumberjack's leg. Badger took the body with him to a nearby alleyway. He dumped the body in a wide-open window! although someone had seen Booming Badger!

Booming Badger hid in the nearest trash can, but the person who saw him immediately called the cops. The cops arrived and Booming Badger was on the run.

He hopped in his driver's car and said go fast. The cops were shooting right at Booming Badger, but Badger was shooting back at them too. Booming Badger shot a bullet straight into the cop's driver of the car, and they crashed.

Booming badger got away with murder! He headed back to his hideous hideout and bought some expensive stuff.

The Fox and the Hawk

By Riley Moore, Aged 9

Fox was strutting, as he always did, when down flew a hawk from out of the sky.

Fox shouted, "Retreat! Retreat! A hawk attacking!"

Fidget the Fox heard no reply, so he ran straight into his burrow to see, but there was no whisker to be seen! He shouted and screamed, asking for help.

Still no reply. He realised that the covers of the beds and everything else had been shredded to pieces. Fidget went back outside and saw that the hawk had gone and there were a trail of fox tracks leading further into the forest!

He decided to go further in and investigate more about it. As he wandered deeper into the forest, the mighty warrior realised that he was alone. The only sights around him were those of trees and green. Then, he saw something rectangular and unusual – like it did not belong. A sign stuck to a tree that said: 'donut entr the Misteerius cave'. He was most aggrieved about the ridiculous spelling of the sign, but could just make out what it meant. The fox ignored the sign, worried about his family more than danger warnings with bad spelling. He went into the cave to realise there was just a glimpse of light. Before Fidget got any further, he heard a voice of a familiar creature. "Well, well, well, look what we have here. Could you not see the sign?".

Immediately Fidget replied, "well, I could but I couldn't read it very well."

It was the hawk.

In a cage, Fidget saw his whole family. His thirteen sisters, his twelve brothers, his mum and dad, the lot. He ran and ran towards the cage, leaping and flying over rocks. The Fox warrior got to the cage and realised it was an illusion.

"Where are my family?"

"Down here!"

Fidget was about to say, "What do you mean?" but before he could the floor opened up beneath him and he fell into a big pit! He got up, found a torch, picked it up and found a secret passageway.

He continued and saw a real cage with his real family in and they screamed, they cried, so happy that Fidget saved them. The saviour got them out of the cage and found a ladder leading to the surface. They all got to the top and saw the hawk standing in front of them. Before the hawk could say anything, Fidget slid underneath him and found his blind spot and with one swift swipe, the hawk fell to the ground.

The bird got arrested by the fox police and the family of foxes built their home back up and started a new career saving the world. They were called the Ferocious Foxes and they were so famous that even humans knew of them, although they were not entirely sure that the tale was true.

Foxy and Toad's Adventure

By Sebastian Coley, Aged 9

Foxy was in her bed one morning when she heard a bang. So she got out of bed and went outside. Foxy saw that the trees were grey and shrivelled and she was scared. So she ran over and went to her friend's house. Her friend was a Toad, so she opened the door and Toad said "Hi Foxy did you hear that bang this morning?"

Foxy replied with "Yes! What does it mean?"

Toad cried "It means the world is shrinking and you need to dig to the core to stop it shrinking! Also you need to use your builder's suit to smash open the core!"

Foxy questioned "what's a builder suit?"

Toad answered with "It's a suit with a hammer and pickaxe. It's for mining"

Foxy suggested "Let's go outside and get started digging then."

So, Foxy and Toad started looking for stuff like mad. It took them a couple of hours to find a shovel. Then they started digging, they went crazy digging for hours, they couldn't stop!

Until something unthinkable happened; it got hotter and their shovel evaporated. This was because Foxy and Toad had got so close to the core it was just too hot for metal. And they could even see the big rock they needed to crack open.

So they went back up to the surface and it took them over two hours. Finally when they got up to the top,

Foxy cried "How are we going to get something else that won't disappear?"

Toad explained that they need to get an excavator and it's a bit like a bulldozer but doesn't destroy stuff it digs.

So Foxy asked "How are we going to get one if we are in England not America?"

Toad answered with "We use our teleport powers which we can only use twice in a lifetime but whatever you touch teleports with you. Also I can touch you and you will teleport with me then I will have one teleportation left but then you can sit in the excavator touch me then you teleport!"

Foxy added "so we will only have one teleportation power left and we will have the excavator."

Toad remarked "Foxy yes, you're so clever."

So that's what they did when finally after hours of testing it they got the excavator down the hole then in one scoop of the dirt they fell down into this mysterious dungeon.

All over this big boulder it says smash this to open to stop the world from shrinking.

"So, let's use our builder suit and smash it open so we can get back to our lives!" insisted Foxy.

So they broke it open and they saw a flash of light then it was over!

Foxy was in her bed one morning when she woke up terrified.

"Oh, it was just a dream!" sighed Foxy.

The End

The Strange Talking Hedgehog

By Ted Edwards

One Monday a boy named Jake set off on an adventure to find a hedgehog but it wasn't just a normal hedgehog it could talk so he set off into the forest to find one.

But it wasn't so easy there were some evil humans after it as well. So Jake lets Mrs Tinky Winkle live with him until it was safe to venture back into the forest and their goal now is to defeat the evil humans.

The next day to attract the evil humans they put a fake hedgehog that they made out of paper. But it wasn't that easy to attract the evil humans, they were smart enough to know it was bait. So they get into a fight with the evil humans.

They put up a good fight but eventually it came to an end when Mrs Tinky Winkle uses her spikes to defeat them. In the end the evil humans got really hurt and ran away. Also Jake got a massive paycheck of £600,000,000 because the evil humans were the worst villains in the country.

And they end up with a great life and everyone loves and respects them now and Mrs Tinky Winkle could go back into the forest with her family.

The Tale of Little Tawny

By Elizabeth Potter

Little Tawny is the size of a wood pigeon. He is a UK bird. The tiny bird lives in one place their whole life. Once they find their home, they live there forever. They are very shy and quiet.

Once upon a time there was a tawny owl called Tawny and his family, his mother and father. They lived in a tree. When Tawny was really happy his mother called out "Tawny!"

Tawny ran, they went to bird hospital and out came a chick! Tawny was soo happy until they got home the chick got all the attention. He does every single thing. When there were adults he still did everything. He had enough so he moved out.

He found his tree, he lived happily, he found the bird of his dreams and they lived happily ever after.

To Hoppy

By Amelia Dinsdale, Age 6

I have a naughty rabbit called Hoppy.

Hoppy hides in my house!

He loves to cuddle me and we go out together, and he helps me when I'm sad. I love him lots because he makes everything better!

Love you Hoppy!

From Amelia

The Butterfly Moth

By Amelia Richardson

Part One

The Realisation

Fluttering around in the cold moon, the bright lights held up by metal, I cling to the warm feeling. The bright posts are the only thing that makes me warm, I can't see my wings but I bet I am colourful.

I have no idea why people ignore me but pay so much attention to other butterflies. I just want to be loved. I just want to be tested.

I remember my old life before I had to go in my chrysalis and turn into myself now. My old life was good. People paid attention to me when I was a caterpillar.

But one day I saw my reflection and I was horrified that I was a moth! I was never a butterfly, my life has been a lie!

Part Two

The New Life

Once I had found out that I was a moth, after a couple of days I got over it. I started going out in the day (it was way warmer). Some real butterflies came over and asked why a moth like me was out during the day. I told them that I want to be a butterfly instead of a moth. They told me that they would help me, one butterfly even said that I could stay with her (Bella).

After a few months (three) I started to fall in love with Bella. I asked her out and she said yes! I was overjoyed. Unfortunately, only a few months later Bella died.

My life was over and my lover was dead…

Junk Escape

By Lucille Teasdale, Age 7

Emily and Maddie were collecting junk modelling for the topic they were doing at school. Bob (their dad) was helping to find the hidden 'treasure' (random recycling) that Rosie (their mum) had hidden for them to find. Later that day, Emily had found a box from Edward's nappies. Meanwhile Rosie hanging up the washing while listening to Boris the Blackbird.

Boris was a small blackbird with a bright yellow beak and a white spot next to it. Rosie loved Boris. She named him because he came to the garden so often. She knew it was Boris because of the white spot. Being outside made Rosie feel really calm and relaxed listening to the sound of Boris.

The next day Maddie and Emily set off for school and on the way they spotted Boris. But, he wasn't quite as familiar because there was a yellow glow coming out of him.

"What?!" said Emily "Err, Maddie!" she said when she saw what was happening to Boris. "Something weird is happening to Boris! Come see!"

"That is truly weird," agreed Maddie when she saw what was happening to Boris.

"Ok, let's stay with Boris," said Emily.

"No, we need to get to school!" Said Maddie.

"Yes, we need to get to school," said Emily. "Can't be late!"

***

"Look what I made!" said Maddie at the end of the day. She had made a rocket and Emily had made a space shuttle.

"Let's go home," Maddie said. "It's Edward's birthday."

"Oh yeah," said Emily.

When they got home they all had some cake and told the story of Boris and the yellow glow.

"Maybe Boris is a magic bird," suggested Bob.

"No way," said Maddie. "There's no such thing as magic!"

They were standing in their models when Rosie called the girls. "Come see Boris! He's in the garden!"

"Ok! We're coming!" they called.

"Hi Boris!" the two girls would say when they saw Boris in the garden.

"Can we ask you why there was a glow coming out of you?" asked Maddie.

"Ah, that glow is very powerful. The glow is my magic."

The two girls glanced at each other. "But it can't be. It doesn't exist."

"Of course it does," laughed Boris. "I am from a different galaxy. I can give you power to work those rockets and shuttles."

"That would be brilliant," said Emily.

So Boris gave the rocket and shuttle some power to work properly. They decided to make another rocket and shuttle for their mum and dad and one for Edward too.

"Come back soon Boris," they said as Boris fluttered away.

When Boris came back they had the space vehicles ready in the garden so Boris could put some magic in them. The next day they went to the shops to get food when Emily spotted some space suit pajamas.

"We need some space suits, then we could really go to space!"

"Ok," said Bob and Rosie. "We'll get them."

The next day they climbed into their rockets and shuttles(even Edward)! Then they said "3, 2, 1, lift off!" and shot into space!

It got darker and darker until Maddie said "I think we're in space now."

"I agree," said Emily, and indeed they were in space because Rosie said "I think I see the International Space Station."

"Me too," said Emily.

Ahead of them, they saw a planet. The planet was pink with blue polka dots and lots of jungle that was especially teeming with life. Most of the life was blackbirds and the rest of the life was Aledlus. Aledlus wore everything to match with their planet. Their head, body, arms and legs matched the colours of the planet they lived on.

"Oh wow," said Emily when she saw it.

"Do you know something," Rosie said. "I think this is Boris's planet."

"Oh yeah," said Maddie. "With all the birds on."

"They all have that white spot," said Emily. They all headed for the strange planet and finally they landed. They all bounced with joy. They started striding through the jungley path. Then Maddie spotted lots of treehouses.

"I wonder if that's where the Aledlus live."

And indeed it was.

"I think we will go home now, because we will frighten all the Aledlus," said Emily. They did go home, or else they would frighten the Aledlus

They contacted the Guinness world-record company to say they think they broke a world record and they did! Edward got the world record of being the youngest person in space, and they were very grateful to Boris.

The End

Fluffy the Otter

By Felix Hutchinson, Age 7

When Fluffy the Otter was born, he could never do things like his friends, because he could not swim nor catch fish or run very fast and he wanted to do those things properly so he went down to the river to try and swim. At first he just paddled his paws in it because beaver had said that before you swim you should always paddle your feet in the water to test if it is hot or cold. It was in between so he went a bit further and he had to hold onto a stone because the current nearly washed him away.

He saw a minnow, just a few yards away but the only thing was, he could not swim so he could not catch it. Sadly he wandered out of the river wishing he could swim.

Just then he saw Beaver, and Fluffy went over to him.

"I can't swim," said Fluffy. "Can you teach me?" Fluffy said.

"Of course I will," said Beaver, so they went down to the river.

"Come in," said Beaver, so Fluffy did.

He went further and further until he was so far he just had to grab a rock and go back to the shore. Every day Fluffy went back to the river to try and swim, he got better every time. Then one time he did it perfectly, so he went to tell Beaver.

"Well done!" said Beaver.

"I'll show you!" said Fluffy. So they went down to the river. Fluffy dived into it, and then Beaver, because he wanted to join in the fun.

"Excellent!" said Beaver.

It was starting to get dark, so they said 'bye!' and went back to their homes.

The next day he wanted to start catching some fish so he went down to the river. Just then he saw a school of minnows, and he tried to catch them but they were way too fast. Later on a bigger fish came. Fluffy dived in and grabbed it. He dragged it out of the water and he went to look for leaves and twigs so that they could have a feast. He went to find Beaver and they started eating.

"So you caught your first fish," said Beaver.

"Yes!" said Fluffy.

"Nice work!" Beaver said, and when they had finished Fluffy went back to the river, he saw some minnows, then he opened his mouth and ate them. He now knew how to catch fish.

Now all he wanted to know was how to run fast, he started running as fast as he could, then he started racing his friends but tripping over rocks and learning to dodge them.

"I think I should start the animal Olympics!"

Survivor

By Lily Mei Rowe

"Many animals are regularly killed, for people's entertainment! This happens to animals like us, pheasants, foxes, badgers and others."

"Is it true?"

"Yes, it is," said Uncle Deer sadly.

"That's really bad, I hope we stay safe!" exclaimed Baby Deer.

In the morning, all the deer went to have breakfast and trotted outside for a run.

"Yay! It's autumn!" shouted Baby Deer.

"Yes, isn't it beautiful?" said Daddy Deer.

Baby Deer asked Mummy Deer if he could go to the river. Baby Deer then trotted to the river on a frosted path through the beautiful red, orange and yellow autumn leaves. Baby Deer ate some herbs, then smelt an unusual scent coming from the meadow's direction. The sound of thunder boomed from across the meadow, echoing all over the forest. All the deer ran to the safety of the forest.

Baby Deer stood in shock as the peace was shattered, then quickly turned, fleeing deeper into the forest. Mummy Deer saw Baby Deer run quickly towards her. She sighed with relief, asking worriedly where he had been. Baby Deer explained he had only went to the river and asked "where is dad?"

She turned and looked at her son!

More than three million wild mammals are killed every year, 15 million birds are shot, and 20 million mice and rats are killed in Britain. Sadly, these terrible things still happen today in Great Britain. Even though some of these things are illegal, people still do it, so let us save the British wildlife.

The Sleepy Lizard

By Emily Edwards

There once was a lizard named Jeffery, but he liked being called Jeff. He was very chilled and he was always sleeping . He was sleeping by the museum. He was sleeping by the school. He was sleeping on a train track. He was sleeping by the pool!

But then, as he was about to drift off to sleep, it was like the world started spinning. Another lizard caught his eye. He walked up to her and asked her if she wanted to go on a midnight walk with him. She replied that she would.

They walked and held hands and they didn't even know each other's names! But eventually he found out her name. It was Violet. It was the most amazing name ever! When it was time to go, they did a big hug but then she disappeared into midair. Unluckily for Jeff, it was all a dream.

The End

Eva and Eve, the Scientists

By Felicity McMurtary

Chapter One

The beginning of a lifetime dream

Once upon a time there lived some scientists called Eva and Eve. They were best friends and they loved singing together "best friends for ever, best friends for ever" as they held each others hands.

***

One warm morning they went for a photography walk. Suddenly, as they both peeped through the berry bushes full of fruit that looked perfect to pick and make into delicious jam, they both gasped and widened their eyes at the whole thing, there was so much wildlife, animals and flowers. It was so beautiful and amazing.

There were rabbits and butterflies, yellow and red poppies and tulips scattered everywhere. Their minds were blown, it seemed too good to be true like a dream, and they froze with amazement and then they soon came running towards the field to explore the grassy jungle around them. There was too much to do in just one day.

For days and days they studied, finding more and more interesting information about the wildlife around them. They found that sheep were scared when other animals attempted to enter what they counted as their territory. Interestingly, they didn't mind the bees, butterflies and ladybirds crawling around them. It was just, the bigger animals like wolves which every now and again came in the middle of the dark, dark night.

Eva and Eve lived in tents in that good old grassy field, there were just so many facts they could learn.

"I love this," said Eva.

"This is amazing," said Eve.

But then as they turned their heads, they suddenly saw in the corner of their eyes an animal trapped under the wooden fence crying with pain and what was even worse was as they got closer, they realised it was a sheep giving birth and it was struggling!

All of a sudden they both started thinking like mad, trying to think up an amazing plan in their science brains to help the struggling sheep - but they just couldn't think. But anyway, they kept on running towards the struggling animal hoping they could work out what they needed to when they got to the floundering animal.

Chapter Two

Working together to make dreams come true

They both helped the sheep by calming the sheep down and lifting up the fence. Then they helped it give birth. It had three baby lambs. Eva and Eve even fell a bit in love with the newborn, trembling, fragile, cute baby lambs!!!

Eva and Eve stayed in that field, learning about the wildlife, and helping the plants and animals if there were any problems.

And as their wildlife exploring expedition came to an end, they both waved a farewell, sang "best friends for ever, best friends for ever", kissed and hugged and went back to their own labs having lived together for 2 years. Every now and again they went together to the field to see how the wildlife was getting on, and how the lambs they helped had grown up, and had lambs of their own.

Their research has helped other people know actually how friendly and in need of help wildlife is. They even made a group of their own about helping wildlife.

Adventures of a Common Lizard

By Thomas Potter

Hiding in the trees, a common lizard can be seen. Scared of their prey in case they get killed, they are about to start running away. It is wagging its tail, making room. It has been spotted by a different animal. Good thing it is super good at climbing – and off it goes! Up into the tree in under one second. Camouflaging into the leaves, hiding from the giant, scary lion. The common lizard is now leaping from tree to tree and now has leaped onto the grass and is running for its life. It has now managed to get into a small tunnel!

The common lizard is safe from the gigantic, terrifying animal or rather, lion. The lizard is now walking on all fours down the tunnel, as happy as he has ever been before. While walking down the tunnel, he has found the exit which brought the common lizard to some type of tropical forest with dinosaurs like a t-rex and pterodactyl. But there is one problem – the tunnel he came from is blocked by a huge rock.

The common lizard thought of a plan, to crawl or climb under the rock. The common lizard is so small but the only problem with the plan is that the dinosaurs have seen the common lizard. The common lizard is trying to squeeze under the rock which is very hard because it is only just his size.

The dinosaurs were on a charge and now right behind the common lizard, chomping its jaws. The common lizard was about to get eaten but managed to get under the rock and escape the dinosaurs. But, the dinosaurs picked up the rock and chucked it away like it was a feather. The common lizard then sprinted into the tall tunnel and ran away as fast as it could go.

The Story of Lila Skyfox

By Clara Sutherland

How it all Began

It all began the day before Lila's birthday and she was practically bouncing up the walls. Lila was seven years old and she had a twin sister named Kitty. As dawn approached Kitty got ready with her surprise gift for Lila, it had been a secret all until now.

Kitty and Lila's favourite animals were cats so that explains why Kitty's present was a kitten called Lulu, the Siamese kitten was a very friendly and trustful cat while being a little bit of a scaredy cat at times.

As Lila's eyes opened she sleepily got out of bed not realising it was her birthday and then suddenly she said suspiciously "Wait... why are you in my room?"

"You stupid duh brain, we're in your room because IT'S YOUR BIRTHDAY!!!"

And that was the signal to mum and dad to start the song. "Happy birthday to you," they cheered happily "happy birthday to you!"

"Happy birthday dear Lila, happy birthday to you...."

They finished just as Lulu walked into the room with a paper crown and a tiny purple cape.

Kitten Mischief

Lulu heard his owners arguing. "Why can't they just live peacefully?!" He muttered frustratedly waking up from his morning nap.

"Oh, now look what you've done! Lulu was having a nice quiet snooze and you've just woken him up!" Lila screamed madly at Kitty.

Maybe I should root in the trash cans… even that's more peaceful! thought Lulu!

So he wandered out the cat flap as agile as a dragonfly, sliding his smooth silky paws over the rock hard concrete with the soft breeze blowing against his slim, elegant body. Suddenly he twitched in alarm and froze with fear as he spotted a trace of soft amber fur glinting in the moonlight...

He knew it, it was a young fox. It circled round him dipping her head, which meant she respected him, and then she said "I'm VixenGrin- call me Vixen for short- and I have something to show you."

Lulu shuddered in surprise while he followed the sly fox to the terrifying woods.

"This place is hidden and you need to use your eyes to find it."

Suddenly Lulu was transformed into a peacock. He tried to hiss in alarm but, he couldn't!

"I'll join you if you find it," and with that the sleek fox slid away from the scene and Lulu searched for hours before he stopped.

"Wait, if I'm a peacock then how has that got to do with it? …Ohh I get it, it means the "eyes" on my back feathers... I need to show them!"

So he ruffled up his big fluffy tail until it was a splendid show of beautiful feathers then suddenly he was transformed into a cat and was teleported into a magnificent castle full of light.

VixenGrin teleported to him using the strength of this magical place to find him. "This is my home," she smiled.

Lulu just stood there gobsmacked as the peacocks invited him further into the blazing beams of light, giving him a fresh rabbit to snack on. He asked them if animals came to their palace often and they said no, because no one was clever enough to find it. So Lulu said he'd visit every now and then. "But as long as I don't have to stay a peacock forever," they all chuckled when he said that. They all had happy lives afterwards.

The Camping Trip

By Alexander Doupe, Age 9

This is a true story, although no-one thinks it is, and you probably won't believe me either. But you should, because it could save your life one day! The story begins with a camping trip on the Lambton Estate, on the bank of the River Wear.

The trees were still as statues, and towered over us. Small animals were scurrying on the ground and nimbly climbing the trees. The sky was clear and blue. The River Wear was calm and its water reflected the forest, like a shiny mirror. I was lying on my sleeping bag in the tent. I was supposed to be playing with my younger brother, Jonathan, but I was more interested in reading my book about the folklore of County Durham. I didn't want to go on this camping trip because I'm really more of an indoor person.

Jonathan was destructively throwing stones into the river.

I had finished reading so I got out of the tent to play with my brother.

Jonathan threw the biggest stone yet. There was a loud bash as the stone fell to the bottom of the lake. After a few seconds, it was no longer peaceful.

The river now had waves violently crashing against the rocks. The savage wind uprooted the trees, now hanging on for dear life.

"What's going on?!" asked Jonathan, bewildered.

"I don't know!" I shouted. "Maybe the fish are angry because you've thrown those stones!

A lightning bolt struck, and out of the water came an enormous, 40-foot snake. It opened its large mouth to reveal dagger-like teeth and a long forked tongue. Its back was covered in spikes like curved thorns. Its scales were jet black, and its eyes were a deep yellow. It had nine holes on its forehead. It hissed loudly, slithered out of the river and curled around the nearest hill.

"Funny looking fish," said Jonathan.

"Jonathan… That. Is. Not. A. Fish!" I replied furiously.

The beast spotted us, uncurled from the hill and began slithering straight towards us.

We turned and ran. My heart was beating so hard that it felt like it would explode.

I dived back into the tent but to my horror Jonathan was no longer with me. Where was he? Had the monstrous serpent got him? And what was it?

And then I realised; the answer was right in front of me. The monster on the front of my book was the same as the one we had just seen. I turned the pages rapidly to find what this creature was. I found it in the tale of John and the Lambton Worm. The Worm was a fearsome beast who terrified the people and ate sheep and children. And we were in the exact spot where the worm was killed!

Why hadn't anyone warned us about the Lambton Worm?

There was a rustle in the bushes near the tent. The Lambton Worm was slithering into the tent. It opened its monstrous jaws, and snapped with force.

Silence. I woke up with a start. I had fallen asleep while reading. It had all been a dream. Nothing but a dream.

Or had it?

Where was Jonathan?

My fist was clenched.

I opened it to see a jet-black scale.

The Snail's Big Day

By Aaliyah Webster

One sunny day, a very lonely and sad snail was sliding its way through the woods. There was a poster on the tree and it said:

BIG NEWS:
ANIMAL RACE DAY
COME AND JOIN IN!!

The snail thought to himself; *there would be no chance that I will win this race, but it's worth having a go.*

Suddenly the snail heard little footsteps behind him and all of a sudden there were two little rats. The rats both saw the poster and they looked at each other and nodded. The snail made his way to the start of the race. All of the animals were gathered around at the startline. There were hedgehogs, tortoises, hamsters and other woodland creatures.

Once all the animals were ready, they all looked at each other very competitively. They nodded their heads as the race was about to start.

There was a red squirrel in a tree, and he shouted "go!".

They were off! One of the animals was a male white rabbit, who was very fast. He was so fast that he got halfway around the course in a very short time, and all of a sudden felt very hungry. He was so hungry he had to go find some food immediately.

The two rats in the race were big-headed, and they thought they were very fast. The rats thought they had time for a quick nap and it would not matter. The lonely snail was still very far behind on the course, after one hour of sliding through the forest.

The snail passed the two rats lying asleep against the tree. He felt like waking them up but in the back of his mind he wanted to win. So he carried on, making sure not to wake the rats up.

Another three hours had passed in the race. The snail was approaching the finish line, but he was so tired and hungry that he felt like giving up. But the lonely snail knew that if he kept going a little while longer, he would reach the finish line.

After ten more minutes of sliding through the forest, the lonely snail finished the race. The lonely snail looked around for other animals that were in the race. He couldn't see the white rabbit or the two bigheaded rats, or any other animals that were participating.

He thought to himself, *where could they be?*

He soon realized that he was the only one there. He thought, *am I the only one here? I think I have won the race?*

Just as he realized he had won the race, the white rabbit came running past the finish line. The white rabbit had found some food but had completely lost track of time. He was closely followed by the two big headed rats who were no longer sleepy.

The lonely snail felt very proud of himself and he had finally achieved what he thought was impossible. Once all the animals that had entered the race had finished, they couldn't believe what the lonely snail had achieved. They all congratulated him, and they all agreed with perseverance and focus that anything could be possible.

The lonely sad snail was not lonely anymore; he was now the most popular snail in the forest.

Bob the Boar

By Rose Wilson

There was once a boar named Bob. He enjoyed being grumpy at the fair, at the park, in the house and by the ice cream van. One day he met another wild boar named Bobolina and he fell in love with her. She had fallen in love with him.

They eventually got married and had baby boars called Billy and Bobby.

When the kids were 9 years old, there was a Climate Crisis. Their home had been destroyed like so many animals' habitats. They decided to meet up with Jeff the lizard and his family.

The three children played together whilst the adults discussed the problem. They decided to go and tell the humans how much they were hurting the environment.

The humans didn't understand the animals but they stopped hurting the environment.

The End

By Poppy Catton

I walked along the woods, not a sound could be heard, the sky was dull and there was no-one around. Until I heard a rustling in the bushes which caught my attention.

BANG!

What was that?

I'm scared now so I begin to run. I can hear my heart banging faster and faster every second.

I was running out of breath. Oh no, I couldn't do this. I have asthma and faint often when I run out of breath. I searched my pockets for my inhaler but it was nowhere. If I fainted here that would be the end. No-one was around, no-one. I could fall, hit my head, and get seriously injured.

No!

I had to run home no matter how hard it was. I needed to be safe, I needed someone to help me.

"Mooooo…"

A cow? Is that what that was? Or was it a person trying to trick me? In the distance I saw a cow trotting towards me; it was real.

"Moooo!"

I heard it again, louder this time as the cow came closer to me.

Suddenly I heard lots of animal noises, crickets and birds chirping, ducks quacking, chickens squawking, bushes rustling and fish splashing in ponds, even though there are no ponds around.

I didn't even realise that two cows were standing either side of me. One of them looked at me then picked me up onto the other one. I was moving. Was this real? Was I hallucinating?

But I was moving! I knew I was!

I lay back on the cow and looked up at the sky. It was magical, like something I'd never seen before. The clouds formed small people and lots of magical creatures.

Ouch, my head was pounding. It appeared my eyes were shut, so I forced myself t open them.

"She's awake!" is all I heard.

Mum…? Dad…? What happened? They looked at me; I'd said that out loud.

"Daisy, you fainted whilst on your walk earlier."

"No I didn't! I was riding a—oh…"

I looked around. Hospital. I knew this place too well, like the back of my hand.

I felt really bad for myself because I kept my parents here really late, worrying. "Sorry, thank you for helping me."

"Don't thank me, thank Bob!" my mum said. Bob was my next door neighbour.

It was late by that time. It must have been around 10pm, so I went to sleep.

I don’t remember very much since then, but I remember seeing Bob and thanking him, giving everyone hugs and drifting away.

This time my eyes didn’t open.

Peanut

By Emily Bell

Once there was a squirrel named Peanut. Peanut lived with her mum and dad in a small hole inside an oak tree, and even though she was only small, she loved to explore. But there was one place she couldn't go and her parents had banned her from ever going there.

Peanut couldn't understand why she couldn't go there so she decided to confront her parents and ask them why she wasn't allowed to go there. So she went up to her mum and dad and said to them "Why can't I go across the river and to the other side of the forest?"

"Because," said her mother, "it is dangerous there, and I don't want you to ever go there!"

This made Peanut very angry because all she wanted to do was explore and her parents wouldn't let her go, so one night she came up with a plan. She was going to sneak out and try to see what was on the other side of the river.

It was now midnight, and Peanut's parents were fast asleep, so she decided that now was the perfect time to escape. So she tiptoed out of her home and down through the trees until she reached the river. In the river was a log, but it was going to be a big jump if she wanted to reach it. So she channelled all of her courage and leaped down from the tree and towards the log. But there was one thing she hadn't planned for, and it was the fact that the log was moving!

So she leaped through the air and missed the log completely. She ended up falling into the river and she began to panic because she couldn't swim!

"Help… help!!" yelled the squirrel as she struggled to stay afloat.

Just as she thought all hope was lost she could see her mum and dad coming towards her. Peanut had never been so relieved in all of her life. Her parents both grabbed onto a stick and reached out towards Peanut. She then grabbed onto it and they both pulled her out of the water.

"The reason we didn't want you going across the river is because of how dangerous this river is!" said her parents.

"I'm really sorry," apologized Peanut. "I'll never go there again."

And from that day on she swore to always listen to her parents, even if it seemed unfair, because they were only trying to keep her safe.

Toby's Terror

By Alfie James

In the afternoon, after a family of foxes had finished their feast on a chicken the father had found in the farmer's backyard, he started to get ready for another heist.

The next day, he didn't come back, so the family thought he had run into a problem. His son Toby waited for three days knowing that he would have to hunt, but deep down he knew he was gone.

So Toby went out to search for him, only to find him dead on a fence coated in barbed wire, just hanging off, along with the only entrance in blocked. Now knowing, he knew he had to make a way in to steal some food with no help and no clue what to do.

So, not knowing what to do, he ran home as he also ran through his memories of him and his father. Not knowing where he was going, he tripped on a root and fell down the edge of a cliff, and landed on some snow unconscious.

He woke up in his consciousness, greeted with a gate the size of a house and a sealed lock. Suddenly eyes appeared in the dark and a reflection of him walked out surrounded by a red aura. He then spread apart six tails and explained to Toby that he was a 10,000 year-old demon fox that had been sealed inside of him by his father.

Black Beauty and Me

By Katie Park

As I woke up the glorious sun shone through my bedroom window. The birds tweeting and bees buzzing made me jump with joy. I quickly got dressed and rapidly ran out of the cottage door just in time to catch the fresh breeze of spring. I looked around and there was a marvellous field of daffodils.

I slowly strode through the field but found a little animal, coated in black and white fur. I suddenly realized what it was, a SKUNK! I ran further and further into the field and reached a forest. The trees were slick brown with luscious green leaves.

Suddenly whilst running through the forest I found a wonderful waterfall, it was surrounded by adorable animals and creatures. I came across a little rabbit. I went to stroke its small head but it rapidly hopped away, taking me to more and more animals. Then there was a beautiful hose, it was the horse of everyone's childhood!

I hopped on its back and the horse galloped into a field with a small pond. Whilst travelling in the field I thought of a perfect name for the horse, Black Beauty. The moment I thought of it I knew it was right. We arrived at the pond and I realised almost every animal had followed us.

I saw my cottage and realised how close I really was to these amazing creatures and fascinating forests. I saw the time and knew it was time to go back so I stroked the rabbit and horse goodbye and headed my way back to the cottage.

After walking for five minutes I reached an enormous rock. I saw a doorway outside of the rock so I walked through and realised it was another way home. I kept running through the halls and reached the end where there was a door and opened it. It was my cottage. I was home.

I then headed back to bed thinking about if this was all a dream so when I woke up the next morning I retraced my footsteps. It was true, I did live in this amazing, gorgeous world. I repeated my day on and on.

Once it had come to the end of the day again I realised all the world had gone gloomy and miserable. I headed to bed realising the upsetting world was true. I wandered back down to the forest and saw Black Beauty lay dead with flowers around it. I walked home upset and never repeated the wonderful day again.

Later in the evening I saw a black figure heading to the cottage. I knew who it was, Black Beauty!

I was overly amazed and rebuilt my home in the forest so I was with my best friends, the animals. I began to love my life so much more and I had never been so happy as with animals and all my friends around me. Finally, more animals came from offspring.

My name is Katie and this is my life!

Otter Alone in a Big Home

By Chloe Longe

One day there was an otter. His name was Scooter. He wasn't the best at being an otter but he got by just fine. He liked to stay inside and swim about as he was antisocial and scared of what life would be like out in the open. Well, at least he thought that because of an incident that happened many years ago, an incident that would change the way his tiny little mind thought forever.

The incident...

Scooter woke up like he did every morning and was about to go see his family as otters do before they go swim and go for their meal, but as he was getting up from sleeping he noticed something, something awful. He was in a weird cave, one that wasn't his own.

He was terrified, letting out shrieks to warn his family they'd been taken, but it was no luck, he was alone. Although he felt upset and in distress he decided he couldn't just sit there mourning.

He should pick himself up and find his family as they were the only thing that mattered to this poor otter.

He quickly scrambled across the ground searching for the exit to this what seemed like never-ending cave. Eventually Scooter saw the light and sped forward ready to fulfil his quest of finding his family but as he got closer and closer it hit him.

Cameras flashed, children screamed and everything felt like danger. He had no idea what to do. He stood in pain, scared for his life. What would happen? Was his family okay? He all of a sudden felt an uncomfortable feeling rushing through his body. Was it over? No. He ran through the cave trying to find his bed.

After the incident...

Ever since that event happened, Scooter felt alone and forgotten. He thought there was no hope in life. He believed that he had died and couldn't do anything anymore.

He was an otter alone in a big home.

The End

The Bee's New Friend

By Connor Whitworth

The bee flew past my house and it was yellow. He liked to fly on the flowers and dance. Then he left for his little hive. Once he went to his hive he started to go to his little friends but he dropped the pollen, so he went to his house and asked his friends to help, but they said no.

A robin sitting in a tree noticed how sad he was and the bird said "why don't I help you get more pollen than your friends?"

The bee said "yes!" in excitement and the bird said "get on my back. I know a flower field near here."

The bee and robin flew for about a minute and landed near a flower, so the bee gathered some pollen and flew back (it was quicker than last time) and flew into the hive. The Queen saw how much pollen there was and she was amazed and promoted the bee to second in command. Then the Queen gave the bird an entire hive (with no bees in) to live in and the bee and the robin were best friends after that.

After watching the bee and the robin, I realized how amazing wildlife is.

The Fox and the Hunter

By Diana Canadas-Ortiz

Carefully she walked through the woods, in her head she told herself 'we will be okay, we will be fine…'

Every time she said the phrase a tear shed down her face. She had just gained the courage to carry on walking through, hoping she would be okay. As she felt the wind hit her, she became paralysed with the feeling that she was caught and had been followed as she entered the woods.

Surprisingly, completely out of nowhere, a fox jumped behind her and as she turned around, she noticed that whatever was making her so scared was most likely gone. The fox stared at her, its eyes very big and bright. It was so young and little with its mesmerising red fur soft as cotton. The fox seemed to have saved her knowing what it was doing. For a split second she had forgotten all of her troubles and began to wonder why this fox had saved her and how did it end up there.

She smiled.

After most animals went extinct in Britain due to hunters going around the towns taking the lives of poor animals, she thought there wouldn't be any wild animals left, so it was very strange how that fox was standing there right in front of her after saving her life.

It had been a few minutes after she had just processed the shock of being in these woods alone, the fox began to walk and without hesitation she followed the fox every step of the way, and with every second more hope.

When they reached the lakes and dangers of the forest this particular fox would somehow save her; it seemed strangely smart, maybe too smart. She had decided the little fox well deserved a name – William. The little girl never quite understood why, but when she looked at the fox she had a feeling as if it was trying to tell her its name was William. They both kept going through the forest, passing through all the dangers.

After a while, the girl felt lonely even with the fox next to her, and she began to consider if the fox could understand English words and meanings so out of curiosity she began to tell the fox how she ended up deep in the woods alone in the night.

"Ummm, hello William. You must be wondering how I ended up here as I assume you've only seen me just being scared of nothing… Well, my mother and I wanted to save as many animals as we physically could from the horrible forest hunters which obviously was quite a big risk."

She had suddenly paused as she remembered what could have possibly happened to her mother. Even though she felt pain explaining all this information to an animal she felt some kind of comfort with that fox so she carried on.

"Well… We tried and I guess it could only work for a matter of time before the hunters began knocking on doors asking for pets, and we noticed when people refused it was a life or death choice. Either the pets die or they die… My mother wanted all to keep safe so we moved to a hidden house on a cliff, but it didn't take long for the hunters to find out about our mini zoo inside our cottage and…"

She began to sob once again, and the fox signalled for her to take a break and sit down for a moment, showing it was truly listening to the girl.

She smiled and hugged the fox with all the love and kindness in her broken heart. "They found out, and my mother risked everything to keep me safe, so she told me to run in here."

The fox closed its eyes and nodded, once again signalling the girl to stand up and keep walking through. They had almost reached the end of the horrible suffering of the woods when the fox realised something the girl hadn't. And as the fox tried to stop the girl from running to the cottage, the girl refused and sprinted straight to her cottage, being followed by the armed hunters surrounding her home.

Her mother was not inside.

Slowly she covered her mouth in pain and shock as one of the hunters pointed a the gun at her. She walked backwards trying to escape but she had failed this time, and in a matter of seconds the fox jumped in front of her, taking the hunter's last bullet and saving her life once again that evening.

She hugged the fox tighter than ever, not letting go and nobody could stop her. Even when the fox was officially gone, she felt its paws hug her back.

Bella the Otter

By Bethaney Blakelock

Hi, my name is Bella, but people call me Bell. I have brown fur on my back and white fluffy fur on the front. I am an African clawless otter that lives beside a lake, and I am here to tell you a story that once happened to me.

Once upon a time, I was going to my bed right next to a lake because that is where I live. So I went to sleep.

5 hours later, I hear a massive scream, I woke up in fear to see a massive strike of lighting right in front of me. I jump backwards and fall into the lake but, like I said before, "I don't swim because I live on land."

So, I fell in and started to sink to the bottom. But then there was a group of animals, otters and squirrels, holding a rope so I could climb up it. But I don't have claws so they pulled me up instead. Luckily I survived but I got a couple of injuries, but they helped me for a couple of days because they didn't get shocked or struck by lightning.

So, it was a happy ending, but just barely, before I could even get out of bed. So you see otters like me are really helpful to other animals but at least I was not by myself.

My friend was the same, he got struck by lightning and nearly got killed but didn't until two months later. He was that sick that he died but I don't think about it because it makes me upset because he was a good friend and I didn't want that to happen. He lived a happy life.

But anyway it was nice telling you my story about my friends (otters and squirrels) were there to help me out.

All of a sudden there was a loud bang outside.

(I stopped telling my story and there was a strike of lightning just outside the window, and we all screamed with fear.)

The Curlew's Story

By Shannon Bertram

Hi, I'm Robin and I'm a Curlew, a type of bird that has a long beak approximately 15cm long. This is my story!

I love eating earthworms but I can also eat leatherjackets, beetles, spiders and caterpillars. I get hunted quite a lot, I have a lot of scars on my wings from foxes and badges. Me and my two chicks live on a cliff near the lagoon down south so predators can't get us there. I have to find beetles or spiders for my chicks to eat every day so they don't starve and die.

It's quite dangerous for me to go out, but I choose to because if I don't, we'll all starve. We collect water from the lagoon. Down in the lagoon, there are a lot of fish and coral. Personally, I think this is amazing and cute.

If we are ever in trouble, we have a Pegasus friend called Ethan, which means intelligent and wise.

One day while looking for earthworms, Sapphire, one of my chicks, comes wounded to me. She says, "we are being attacked."

Leo, my other chick, is trying to fly over with Ethan and is hiding in the woods with us while the humans are searching for us.

We go to the water and clean the wounds and blood off our bodies and search for a new home.

We decide to live in the trees and I start making a nest while Ethan, Sapphire and Leo have a look at the beautiful flowers underneath our tree.

Then Ethan, Sapphire and Leo see Ethan's family.

His mother, April, approaches them while I'm still getting resources for the nest. Then Sapphire shouts "Mother, we have guests!"

I fly down to see who they are.

They introduce themselves. We talk for what feels like hours. We became friends but then it's time to go home. Our life got better knowing that April was an Equine and Queen of the Unicorns and Pegasi. We were never hunted again.

We lived in the Mythical Kingdom with Ethan's family.

2 Years Later...

Me, Sapphire and Leo were called to go to the throne room for an important message. We were invited to become their family due to living with them for two whole years. We were thrilled and accepted the offer.

We lived happily ever after!

The Chase

By Jakey Sutherland

Once upon a time, I was walking through a deep dark forest. I suddenly heard a crack of a leaf or twig. It was a mysterious animal that was hovering around in the woods. I didn't know what it was. I was walking closer and closer and while I was walking I saw the bees and birds and butterflies flying around. I didn't know what was happening. It was like things were coming alive, and then they were going and coming.

Later that day, I came across an empty beehive and bees buzzing towards it. They saw a dead bee and brought it back to life somehow. I was curious, I started walking and saw otters, a whole family of them crawling around trying to protect their family.

I was tiptoeing closer while they were crawling away. They crawled all the way up to their pond.

Two weeks later I went to the exact same pond, they weren't there. I searched all around the forest. They were nowhere to be seen, the otters were nowhere. I went back to the empty beehive and I saw the bees. They were collecting more honey. I saw the queen bee and then, there they were. There, next to the beehive, swimming in a ditch full of honey.

A couple of hours after that, I saw a wild cow, wait no, ox, no horse. I got closer and closer and it turned out it was a life size ant! It was massive! I walked closer and the life sized ant came closer. I sprinted faster than Usain Bolt. I was scared, I didn't know what to do. I climbed a tree and I was terrified. I could see the whole forest from where I was. I could see the otters, the bees and butterflies, everything. I looked up and I saw three pheasants flying around my head.

I slowly climbed down the tree and there it was, around six feet tall. I was so scared I ran and a poof of smoke came from the back of me. I leaped over the otters in the honeypot with the bees buzzing around. I looked behind me and it was there, right behind me. Running further and further to me.

The deer.

It was there right behind me. I sprinted up the tree and waited until sunset to fall. I carefully climbed down and took in my surroundings. I saw a few red squirrels and a couple of curled up hedgehogs. I crawled down on the ground so the deer didn't see me.

I eventually stood up and looked a stag straight in its eyes. I leaped over him and started running, then I realized. I realized what it was. It was… It was… It was a buffalo. I was so scared. It was coming back and forth after me. I ran and ran but still couldn't get away. I didn't see anything, no trees, no plants, no grass, no leaves, no nothing. Only bare ground.

I dug a little hole but still didn't want to get hurt by the 6 foot buffalo. I hurried and hurried. While it was sniffing I dug around three metres down in about five minutes. I started digging across before the buffalo could catch up to me. I dug 7 metres across before he started digging.

Oliver the Otter

By Alara Setirek

Sophie Clarke was a normal 12-year-old girl from Durham. Although she didn't have many friends, she loved art and had many hobbies to keep her entertained. You may be thinking that Sophie has a perfect life for her age-group but you were wrong, and that was part of the reason why she was running away from the place she had called home for so many years.

You may be wondering what she was running away from? The answer to your question was her new step-mother. She was mean, some people may describe her as a villain. When Sophie had first met her she seemed nice enough but as time went on she started to show her true colours.

She began to slow down as she came to a small, peaceful lake and decided to rest there after at least an hour of running. She took out her sketchbook from her blue backpack and began to draw the scenery around her. She wondered where life would take her from here, would she have a new family? New Friends? Only time will tell.

As she continues to draw the beautiful lake, she notices an odd sound coming from behind her.

"Hello? Is anybody there?" she asks as she grabs a stick from the ground, using it as a weapon. She begins to move closer and closer to the sound, her heart beating faster with every step she takes until she finally builds up the courage to peek around the corner and sees…

An otter?

She drops the stick and goes to kneel down next to the animal. The otter moves closer to her and lays his head in Sophie's lap. She smiled to herself as she no longer felt alone. They stay there for a while before Sophie pulls herself from the ground and looks back to the small brown otter. "Goodbye little otter," she says, and goes back to find her backpack and continues walking through the forest.

But, it feels like she is being followed so she turns around and sees that the otter had been following her. "Looks like I'm stuck with you," she sighs, slowing down her pace to allow the otter to catch up. As she continues walking, she feels something tugging on her leg and notices that the otter had a hold of her leg. "What are you doing?" she laughs but he doesn't let go, instead he begins to drag her in the other direction.

Sophie wasn't too sure where the small brown otter was trying to take her, but felt the urge to follow him, so that's what she did.

The moon had risen and Sophie had lost track of time. "What shall I name you?" the blonde girl asks. "How about… Oscar? Or… I know! Oliver!" She decides and the otter nods his head in approval.

"You do realize we're going back to where I came from, right?" she asks Oliver but he just keeps walking. They keep on walking until they get to a brightly lit house and Oliver stops walking.

"Oliver, what are we doing here? This is my house!" she says as the front door opens.

"Sophie? We've been so worried, where have you been?" her step-mother asks with tears streaming down her face. The little girl didn't expect her step-mother to care seeing as she had never seemed to care about her before, so she began to feel guilty about trying to run away from her.

"I'm sorry, I was at my friend Katie's house," she lies.

"Never run off like that again, okay? Come here."

Her step-mother opens her arms to hug her stepdaughter. Sophie wraps her arms around her new mother and turns around to see if Oliver was still there, but he was gone.

Jerry the Squirrel

By Harry Foster

Jerry's back again - please don't question the name, you will never realise just how boring a day without the internet can get. Dark times that was, dark dark times.

Anyway, if I can count that's the… ohhh, 4th time. In one day! This guy, he thinks he can just knock around here and sit on my wall. He doesn't even do anything, sitting staring. I'll just give him a few nuts, it should make him leave eventually.

Picking them out of my pocket, I scatter them one by one across his vicinity. He doesn't pay any attention, but starts to walk, more of a sneak over to my feet. I nearly walked into the wall with hesitation, but then froze and he was tugging on my jeans. Causing a rip, he was pulling. Not aggressively but it almost seems that he is trying to get my attention.

A minute passed and I was still standing there contemplating my movements, as the tugging was getting rapid and more chaotic. Suddenly it stopped and I hear a whine coming from over the river. The squirrel fled at the speed of light. Instinctively I follow Jerry, confused (but slightly relieved) at his disappearance. The powerful noise takes me through the trees, over the stepping stones that divert the gushing water, vaulting a bush and pushing through a pile of leaves – treading in dog muck on the way. Finally, dappled light illuminates a carving in the tree. The devilish eyes gloom onto me.

The amount of distress is unbearable. Minutes have passed and the increasing tone is causing a ringing in my head. I tried to approach, it didn't go horrifically wrong, not amazingly at all though. With the spread of its legs the animal jumps and claws my shirt hanging on for life. I swipe myself to the side, trying to cause minimal harm. Does not work. A bit more thoroughly. Stuck like glue. I suddenly stopped. Pulling out the last two nuts from my pocket, it jumps and wraps around my fingers as I gravitate it slowly to the ground.

That's when I see it.

It must be about 6 cm long. A gushing cut, dripping its blood like a leaky pipe. Suddenly, like a jigsaw, I finished the puzzle. All the pieces fit perfectly together.

Jerry was a distress signal, a flare that was sent to boldly attract the attention of anyone who could help. I was aid to the little creature. It wasn't trying to hurt me, it was protecting itself and Jerry.

Trying to get a squirrel in a cage isn't easy, you know, but with a few peanuts I made it work. A day later and we were out of the vets. It turns out a rabid fox bit my pal's pal. Puncture to the lungs and a broken rib. He's lucky he didn't die out there on the battlefield, my brave little soldier.

Next morning I decided to lay some peanuts on the floor, just to, you know, see what would happen. Running out with no hesitation, I see a bandaged up squirrel bounding my way. As he gobbles, chews and crunches away a sudden stop in the movement gets my attention. A voice, squeaky, faint. Again. And again.

"You know Timothy Jones, you saved my life. Surely there's a way I can repay you."

My name's Timothy Jones.

The squirrel talks. What?

Tweet

By Maise Rose

Once the time came for a tiny owl to be hatched from its egg which was being protected by its mother. The owl's name was Tweet and he had nicely coloured wings with big yellow eyes and a black sharp beak. Time shot past and the owl was growing. Unlike its siblings, it stuck alongside his mother learning and watching what she does.

2 years have passed, and Tweet was flying with his mother. Suddenly, lightning struck!

BANG!

Tweet panicked and flew off to the safety of a tree. He was scared… really scared. Tweet drifted off to sleep, jumping every time thunder banged. The morning came by and there was no sign of Tweet's mother. As he had followed his mother for years, Tweet had learned the best skills to survive and eat and drink. Tweet was starving; he needed to find food and water. Tweet headed to the ground and he started waiting for worms after he found a few, Tweet flew to the river. Tweet's mother taught him to be careful around the river because of the crocodiles. Like his kit, she told him he was careful and got his water. Tweet flew up to the trees.

Months went on and still no sign of Tweet's mom. Tweet wanted to find her; he would never stop looking; he called in every owl he could in hopes of finding her. All the owls start searching, going past rivers and mountains grass, sand and snow. Nothing would stop them. It had been 2 weeks and no one had any signs of her.

Until Tweet had the best idea; he knew his mom loved the flowers and that she went there when she was scared. Tweet flew through the grass all the way to the flower field.

Tweet had arrived and he went through all the flowers to find the secret base he and his mom made when he was young.

Suddenly, Tweet heard noises - the flapping of wings. He rushed towards it and there she was; his mother! She was alive and survived the storm. Since it been so long, he was excited to tell her everything that happened. Tweet had made them a new home! They rushed back excitedly to tell their stories to each other.

Ever since then they stayed living together, just Tweet and his mother.

First line Challenge

All of students at St. Joseph's school in Gilesgate were challenged to use a collection of words, phrases and themes to tell new and unique stories.

The Woodcutter's Farm

By Thomas Parker, Age 9

Chapter One

A woodcutter drives into the damp, wild woodland in a rusty, muddy truck. He was ruining all the beautiful, vibrant bluebells and the animals weren't happy at all! The woodcutter found a spot in the sun and he jumped out of the van and began to chop a tree which alerted all the animals.

Moments before the woodcutter came the wood was bright and vibrant and joy was spread out around the forest. Birds were cheeping and frogs were leaping and bees were pollinating flowers and buzzing around the wood. You could hear the rain hitting off the leaves and the wind brushing against the trees and the woodland was peaceful as ever. But now there was only silence as the man entered the forest.

Whack!

Chop!

Whack!

Chop!

He had destroyed lots of trees.

"This isn't right," whispered the fox to his friends. The man continued to chop trees to build his farm.

9 months later, the woodcutter's farm was fully built. He even had all the animals, cows, pigs, horses, goats and chickens. He also had a sheepdog to guide the sheep into their pen.

4 weeks later, winter arrived at the forest and the trees had frosted over and there was snow on the ground. The snow covered the forest completely. The ground was as soft as a cloud and as white as a sparkling star in a clear sky.

There were crystal-like icicles hanging off the edge of his house slowly melting. The next morning, the woodcutter took his dog for a walk. There was a deep puddle but it had frozen so the man thought it would be safe. But the puddle only had a thin layer of ice and he stepped onto the puddle and the ice cracked like a bone breaking, and he fell through and he was soaking!

He came home feeling very wet and very cold. He sat down with a blanket and watched TV but he was still cold so he went to light a fire to warm himself up. He put on his soft woolly hat and his wet raincoat and he grabbed his axe and went out to find wood. He found a large tree and he started to ***chop***!

Chapter Two

An owl was gliding through the sky with a mouse in his mouth. The owl flew in a hole in a great, beautiful hawthorn tree and took a bite out of its lunch and got interrupted by a

Chop!

Chop!

Chop!

The owl flew out of his house and perched on one of the branches and said in a booming voice "do you mind! I'm trying to have lunch! And this is my home, not some scrappy junkyard where you can do whatever you want! And also, please don't cut my house down or anyone else's!"

The woodcutter grunted and went home rather cold. After 5 minutes he decided that he wasn't going to listen to some stupid owl so he went out to chop the owl's tree.

Whack!

Chop!

Whack!

Chop!

The man lit the fire and started to warm up. 15 minutes later the fire went out and it became cold again. It was 11 O'clock and the man was sleeping.

A few days later the man got bored so he hopped in his truck and went exploring into the wildlife. He squashed lots of flowers and a dragonfly was resting on one and it got ruined.

So the dragonfly flew through the open window and landed on the man's head and piped in his ear "you've squashed my flower that I was resting on because I'm tired. But now I can't sleep because you trampled all the flowers."

But the woodcutter didn't care.

Chapter Three

4 weeks later, the man was cold again but had no logs for the second time. He put on his woolly hat and this time a warm raincoat because he had put it on the radiator. He grabbed his axe and went to chop down some trees. He found another hawthorn tree but this time the tree was huge. But it didn't stop him.

Whack!

Chop!

Whack!

Chop!

As he swung his axe back the sixth time something rattled in the bush next to him. Out jumped a bright red fox. The man dropped his axe as the fox pinned him down.

The fox growled fearsomely "Stop! This great hawthorn tree is the home of many creatures, and if you cut this tree down you could make them lose their home or worse, you could kill them! And I can't let you do that because I'm the leader and guardian of animals who can't protect themselves, and look what you've done to this beautiful place! Also you chopped down the owl's house when he told you not to and you've ruined the dragonfly's home."

Chapter Four

1 week later, the woodcutter had changed completely. He wasn't a woodcutter, he was now an explorer. He planted lots more trees and replaced the ones he had cut down. He decided to knock down his farm and he sold the animals to another farmer for £9,768 and with the money he hired people to look after the forest and to plant more trees, and only cut down trees if necessary.

The forest lived happily ever after.

The Giant who Had a Heart

By Hallie Appleby, Age 8

A great big giant was chopping down the trees - he was taking one tree after another. The animals watched in horror; the fox was leaning towards heading.

The fox was so scared of the giants he hid in the bushes. Finally he built up enough courage to protect the common home of the woodland animals. He snuck up and growled in the Giant's ear.

"I have lived here for all my life and generations of my family have lived here. Since I was a little baby it's been my home and I wish you wouldn't chop my luscious house down. Where will I go? Do you know the forest is dying because of you and lots more people?"

The giant thought for a second and he found that he had a heart.

Explore, not Destroy

By Talisha, Age 9

A giant walked into the wood. He had a giant axe with him and this was not good news for the animals who lived there. Moments before the wood was alive with the beautiful smell of wild bluebells and the sound of owls hooting. You could see the beauty of the trees and the flowers in the sparkling sunshine which was peeking through the trees.

Why would you want to chop the woods down, instead of exploring it?

The giants had come to chop the trees down and build houses. This had to be stopped!

All of the animals came out into the forest and decided to join together to stop the giants from ruining their beautiful home.

A fox ran over to the giants and whispered into the giant's ear "don't chop the trees down because this is our home and we have lived here all of our lives!"

A few minutes later a little rabbit hopped over to the biggest giant and said "please stop this action and leave our home! This forest has more than a hundred different animals living in in it and if it is chopped down how will we find food and how will we feed our families?!"

The giants all stopped chopping and said "we are sorry that we came to your home to destroy it. Please forgive us and we will start to plant new trees and flowers to make your home a beautiful place again."

The animals all cheered and they worked with the giants to build a better world together.

The Giant and the Birch tree

By Zofia Wanecka, Age 9

A giant walked into the wood. Moments before the wood was alive with the beautiful smell of bluebells and the sound of beautiful songbirds. There were wood anemones and beautiful smelling celendines. Small animals, fox, peacock butterfly, black beetle and dragonfly.

Animals live in the birch tree. Fox's home is tunnels and it is home to the rabbits. The giants had come to chop the trees down and built houses in the fun forest. A fox walked over to the giants and whispered into the giants ear "sir do not chop this tree we have lived here many years and we have made it a fancy home. My family and Rabbit's family live here.

Rabbit ran and said "Sir do you not like animals?"

Roe deer said "Don't chop this tree down, it is home to me and my babies.

The giants stopped and so did the animals.

Building a Better Future

By Callum Hardy

A giant walked into the wood. Moments before the wood was alive with the beautiful smell of bluebells and the magical sound of pigeons cooing. The giants had come to chop the trees down and build houses.

A wise old owl flew to the top of a tree and he shouted "*go away from our woods because you are not welcome*!"

All of the other animals gathered around the trees so that the giants could not chop their homes down. The giants began to shout and become angry but more and more animals came to stop them.

All of a sudden, a huge majestic deer walked into the middle of the crowd and said to the giants "This forest is home to all of our families and our children and if you chop the trees down, *where will we live*!?

The giants looked at each other and said "if we work together, we can save the world."

The animals all agreed and they worked with the giants to build a better future for their children and their families.

The Fox, the Chaffinch and Me

By Elodie Ogle, Age 8

A man came to a wood early that morning where peacock butterflies dance, chaffinches tweet on the branches of holly trees and foxes hide amongst the bushes The man came with his van full of rubbish to dump it in the beautiful forest of wonders. He smelled bluebells and wet mud and grass. He saw how the dazzling butterflies danced and the foxes creeped and how the chaffinches chirped and tweeted.

The peacock butterfly fluttered down to the man and landed on his shoulder. She whispered "if you keep on dumping rubbish there will be no more of this beautiful forest of wonders.

The fox tiptoed to the man and growled "me and my family have lived in this beautiful forest of wonders for as long as I can remember. Do not dump rubbish in it."

The chaffinch flew down next to the man and tweeted "only 13% of the UK is covered in woods and forests."

The peacock butterfly said "use your common sense."

The chaffinch said "do you know where we will live if you dump rubbish in this forest, huh?"

The man thought about what the animals had said. He wondered. He said in a deep and thoughtful voice "is this forest really going to be gone, if I dump rubbish in it?"

The animals said in sweet voices "yes! The forest will be gone if you dump rubbish in it!"

The man thought so deeply and so thoughtfully.

He wanted to save the planet but he did not want to get in trouble with his strict, unfair and coldhearted boss, because he can get ugly! The man knew how much trouble he would be in with his boss but he knew what was better for the beautiful lovely looking planet. He climbed in his van with the rubbish in the back and drove off!

The animals were delighted that he chose to drive away with the rubbish instead of dumping it in the beautiful forest of wonders!

P.S. There is no planet B!

The Family's Woodland Adventure

By Sealey Robertson, Age 8

A family adventure into the beautiful bright forest carrying with them a picnic. They saw a peacock butterfly. Then they listened to the birds chirping and the owls hooting. They started smelling the aroma from the beautiful, wonderful bluebells. They wandered away from their delicious lunch leaving the litter behind them.

Moments before the wood smelt so good with the sweet aroma. It was so good to wander bluebell to bluebell, it was so wonderful here with the birds. It was outstanding here, it was the best.

Suddenly a man came with a white van, he went in the back of the van and took his chainsaw. He walked deep into the forest and started cutting down trees! He started to chop the hazel tree down with the owl in it!

"Do you really want to chop down these trees?"

The animals came out and with signs saying stop! But the man didn't listen to the mole saying "stop!" so the butterfly came and shouted "listen to the mole!"

Together they said "you are ruining the trees! We won't have any oxygen then we will suffer... *Stop*!"

The men stopped.

The Great Oak Tree and the Animals

By Valentina Stephenson, Age 9

A man entered the dark, deep forest. He was going to chop some trees down. He drove in a white air polluting van with a sign on the side advertising new, posh homes. He heard owls hooting in the treetops. The wood smelled of all the lovely flowers blooming up… It was spring! He opened his van doors and grabbed his destructive, cruel axe.

Sensing danger an owl came along and hooted “Don’t you care about the animals homes that you are about to kill?”

Then a fox came along and he howled “this is where we live and you are just going to chop down trees?”

Not long later a butterfly came along and he buzzed “this is where I go flower to flower and you are just going to ruin it?”

Then all the animals came out and standing together said “they are right this is where we live and we are not going to let anyone ruin it!”

The man felt sorry and with a heavy heart went back to his planet destroying van.

He then said to himself, looking back into the forest "I'm never going to chop down a tree again." He felt really bad for what he was going to do. He then thought about something and he went back hoping that the animals would still be there. Some animals were still there, so he said sorry. He then went back to his van and drove away. He felt a little bit better.

The Fight for the Forest

By Izabelle, Age 8

One day a man came into the beautiful luscious forest. The man was a worker. He shouted loudly "I'll chop down this tree first and I'll chop three more after!"

There lived a little rabbit in his burrow. There was a black beetle on a leaf and we can't forget about the woodpecker who was pecking at the wood.

The black beetle piped in the man's ear "we need oxygen to live so if you chop down this big beautiful forest you will die."

The beetle was so small that the worker didn't hear him so he walked on by.

Then the rabbit hopped out of his burrow and he whispered "if you chop down the forest how will you be alive?"

This time he heard the rabbit but he didn't see the rabbit, so he walked on by.

The rabbit asked the beetle this "will you join me to stop this man?"

The beetle replied and the answer was yes.

Then a cute woodpecker flew down from a branch. He squawked "if you chop down this tree where will I find my food?"

The woodpecker joined in with the black beetle and the rabbit. They needed to stop what was happening because climate change is happening fast.

Everyone shouted "stop!"

He stopped and said "I'll plant more trees."

So they planted more trees together but the man got fired from his job. He didn't care because he put up a fight for the forest. To this day more and more people have joined the man but the planet is still bad.

In a Moment, Everything Changes

By Abigail Monaghan, Age 8

Moments before the forest was filled with happiness and animal noises. Blossom fluttering off trees and the green leaves fell as the wind blew by. All was happy, none was sad.

Until a man came with a big axe and struck the tree twice. The tree was weak so it fell down. All the animals were depressed and upset because their home was gone forever.

The animals froze and all was silent.

The man chopped more and more trees until a nice family went over and said "what are you doing?"

The man replied "Chopping down these trees for wood and paper."

The woman of the family said "I don't care if I have wood and paper, I only care if these poor animals are okay!"

The man sadly said "is this true? I am killing all the animals?"

The family cried "yes! You are ruining the lives of all these animals who now shall be homeless! Who are you and do you have a heart? *Stop* and *think* about these poor things!"

The man whispered "I'm so sorry I never thought about the animals who shall now be homeless. I won't listen to that man who told me what to do. In fact, I will quit my job and get something related to nature."

The family were really proud of the man and the family discussed about joining the job and they shouted "we will join you!"

All the animals cheered "Woohoo!"

The family and the man worked every day and all night. Together they became a really famous business company planting trees and more trees. They were all over the news winning awards as the best company in the universe for the planet. They inspired people all over the world because of their worldwide success. They became role models to so many and the planet was better than ever.

The family, animals, and man were so proud that they had a party with all the animals of the wood. The animals were really grateful for everything that happened.

In the end the man was a great man who was famous for his greatness.

The Day of the Giants

By Angelin Denny, Age 9

A giant walked into the woods. Moments before the wood was alive with the wonderful smell of gorgeous bluebells and the sound of a woodpecker tapping with its beak on the trunk of an enormous tree. The giants had come to chop the trees down and build houses.

A woodpecker flew over to the giants and whispered into the giant's ear "stop chopping the trees down, this is our home and you are destroying it. How would you feel if I came to destroy your home? Please do not chop the trees down."

A rabbit hopped over and whispered into the giant's ear "stop chopping all the trees down because you are ruining our lives and destroying the lives of all the many animals who are living in the forest."

A harvest mouse squeaked into the giant's ear "stop making houses and help us find a way to make the forest look more better than it was before."

One day all the animals set a trap for the giants. The giants fell into their trap.

The giants said "Help!"

The animals shouted "we will only help if you stop changing the forest!"

The giants said "sorry because we didn't notice all of the animals were all running out of the forest."

That day the giants helped everyone else and began planting new trees and plants.

The Angry Picnic

By Emily Wardle, Age 8

A nice peaceful family went for a picnic, but were they peaceful? The birds were tweeting… until they came. They were chopping down branches and throwing rubbish into the river and disturbing the hedgehog's nests. When they left, they left all their rubbish.

The family were looking up the last hill and they saw a hedgehog and stopped. It squeaked "I have had my baby but you have destroyed my home so I don't have a place to live!"

One little girl shouted "I will help fix the forest."

They went to the car and the girl was excited to help the forest.

The family, continuing their journey through the wood, encountered a deer. The deer said "Please don't cut off branches because the tree will rot and trees give oxygen so we will die."

The little girl's sister changed and said "I want to be like my sister." So they started to protest against the people who drop litter.

The family were camping so they went to bed but they could not sleep with the owl cooing. The owl flew in and it cooed "if you don't stop chopping down trees and dropping litter our planet will be destroyed."

They were so guilty that they started to protest so the world could be right!

P.S. Help the planet!

The Climate Killers

By Ava Jarvis, Age 8

The Happy Homes company came to the woods.

Moments before the wood was multicoloured, lively and amazing. The sun was shining and birds were chirping sweet songs. The dragonflies were dancing.

They could see children chasing bees, butterflies and more.

"So lads," said the big, bad boss. "Let's chop that one down."

The whole wood went silent.

A magical mystical little owl flew to the big boss and hooted "You can not do this to this particular tree otherwise you will regret this. You will get an almighty punishment so just don't do it. I know somewhere inside you, you know that it is the wrong thing to do."

A magical mystical butterfly fluttered down to the man and said "you chop this tree down, where will I spot my food?"

A fox jumped down and howled "I live in this tree but if it is gone, where will I live? This place is beautiful. It is not just a kids' park. It's a home for animals. Put down the axe and pick up the seeds!"

P. S. There is no planet B!

Take Your Litter Home

By Liam Stoker, Age 7

A family venture into the dark peaceful wood and set up their delicious picnic. They eat and chat with the birds tweeting peacefully in the background. The insects buzz from plant to plant. The stunning aroma from the endangered bluebells drifts past. They finish their picnic and began to wander off leaving their litter.

A magnificent colourful peacock butterfly lived in the tall impressive oak tree. It flew down and landed next to the family It whispered into the family's ear "I started off as a tiny egg laid on the leaf of this great oak tree. I hatched into a tiny caterpillar feasting upon the leaves from the trees in this wood until I became a big fat caterpillar. I finally wrapped myself tight into a chrysalis and emerged into a beautiful butterfly! Please take your litter home with you!"

Change of Heart

By Ben Gibbons, Age 8

The man worked at a wood company. He was ordered by his boss to cut down a hawthorn tree to make some fancy houses. That evening he walked into the intense gloomy forest with an axe hanging down his shoulder. He could hear a squirrel scamper up a tree. He could hear the birds tweeting under the moonlit sky. He could smell the fresh grass. Soon he started.

Whack!

Chop!

Whack!

Chop!

It began to get late. He grew tired, so he left and the man said to his boss, "I will finish this off tomorrow."

The next morning he returned and then a beautiful chaffinch who lived in the forest trees swooped down from a branch and landed on his shoulder. He chirped in his ear "sir, if you chop down this tree of wonder you shall get bad luck.

Soon the man fell asleep and was sleeping on it. The man woke up and the man said to his boss, "some noise said that if I cut down this tree, I will get bad luck!"

"Just get some rest," said his boss."

That afternoon the man returned.

A bee buzzed out of nowhere, and buzzed around the sleeping man's head. He hummed "sir do you know if you cut down this tree it might destroy the bees and if the bees die, who can deny how yummy and delicious the honey we make is?"

A squirrel scampered down and whispered in the man's ear "sir this tree is the tree of wonder. Many animals live here. Please don't chop this tree down because it is our home!"

A hedgehog crept out of a bush and whispered in the man's ear "Sir, animals have lived here for longer than me and the other animals, please don't chop this tree down."

A badger slowly went out of a log and growled "Sir, don't chop this tree down because if you do, where will a' find the black beetles for my dinner?"

A wolf came leaping from out of nowhere and roared in his ear "Sir, if you cut down this tree then I will have you for dinner.

The man dropped the axe.

About the Team

Simon Berry

Simon has been an Optometrist for over 20 years. He opened his own community Optometry Practice in 2002.

He gets bored quickly and has lots of little projects to keep life more interesting. One of the ones he is most proud of is the Gilesgate Story Challenge.

He is passionate about books and when flirting with a different career he did try and write a few himself. (None were ever published.) He had a literary agent for a while but they left soon after to become a coffee barista and he lost his contract. He hopes this wasn't because of having him as a client.

Contact Simon at:
simon@simonberry.co.uk

Or visit the Practice website:
www.simonberry.co.uk

Jenny Pearson

Jenny Pearson Jenny Pearson has been awarded with six mugs, one fridge magnet, one wall plaque and numerous cards for her role as 'Best Teacher in the World'.

When she isn't teaching, Jenny is the author of *The Super Miraculous Journey of Freddie Yates*, *The Incredible Record Smashers*, and *Grandpa Frank's Great Big Bucket List* which will be out in February 2022. She is also the co-author of *Tuchus and Topps Investigate* with Sam Copeland, which will be out in June 2022.

Jenny has been shortlisted for the Costa Children's Book of the Year 2020, the Waterstones Children's Book Prize, the Branford Boase, the UKLA Book awards and the Lollies and has also been Waterstones Book of the Month, The Times Book of the Year and Sunday Times Book of the Week twice.

Fiona Sharp

Fiona currently works in Waterstones as a bookseller! Not only does she love to organise book signings from popular authors, she also enjoys arranging book groups for both children and adults. No matter the destination or journey, Fiona can always be found with multiple books squeezed into her handbag!

Not only does Fiona manage to read more than 250 books a year, she has also managed to feature in a short story by one of her favourite authors, M.W. Craven. If you happen to read this great story remember it's only fiction…

Fiona is known for her recommendations, but be warned customers rarely leave with only a few books and their bank account happy!

Fiona loves to spend a night or weekend at a book event and was even lucky enough to have afternoon tea, in London, with Tayari Jones, author of An American Marriage, and her publishing team.

Finally, Fiona was very proud last year to be nominated as a bookshop hero by two authors, William Shaw & Helen Cullen.

Find Fiona's reviews here (if you dare!):

independentbookreviews.co.uk

Miles Nelson

Miles is an independent author from Durham. Whilst he loves to tell stories of his own, his favourite thing in the world is to help and inspire young writers to hone their skills.

Miles specializes in young adult and children's fantasy, although he has a special soft spot for nature writing. His first book, entitled *Riftmaster*, was released in 2021. It tells the story of a college student who is whisked away from Earth by a mysterious force called the Rift, and encourages readers to find joy in the unknown.

An interesting fact about Miles is that he enjoys collecting books about animals, from the fantastical to those we see every day.

Contact Miles:

milesnelson1997@outlook.com

milesnelsonofficial.com

@Probablymiles on Twitter

Esther Robson

Retired and still loving books so it's been a joy to be involved with the Gilesgate Story Challenge again this year. "Can you read me a story Granny?" have been my favourite words during lockdown! I've not truly mastered the art of reading a book on FaceTime but it's been very entertaining trying and my 3 year old grandson, living in Amsterdam and already developing a huge love of books, sits very attentively.

It's been great fun reading this year's entries. I'm astounded by the imagination of the children and can't wait to read the winning story to my little grandson, Bunny, his name coincidentally in keeping with this year's competition theme!

Acknowledgements

There are so many people to thank for the part they played in creating this book. Everyone is a volunteer and the time and effort they have all put in is humbling and much appreciated.

Thank you, **Miles,** yet again for your amazing work typesetting and illustrating our book.

Thank you, **Esther**, for keeping everyone organised, informed and on time.

Thank you so much to our guest judges this year, **Jenny** and **Fiona**.

Thank you, **Waterstones Durham**, for again supporting our project.

Thank you, **New College Durham** and especially **Clare Dickenson**, for helping us find illustrators to bring these stories to life. See the student illustrators overleaf!

A BIG thank you to all the **teachers, parents, carers, brothers, sisters** and **friends of our authors**. Anyone who has encouraged someone to write their story and send it to us.

But most of all… thank you to all the **authors**. You are all amazing - keep writing and telling your stories!

Illustrators

There were so many people who worked together to bring this book to the shelves, many of whom gave it brightness, colour, and brought the stories within to life.

The lead illustrator on this project was Miles Nelson. He illustrated *Sammy the Useful Slug* along with all the black and white title illustrations that appear throughout the book.

However, many of these illustrations were made by the incredibly talented art and design students from New College, who are listed below in order of appearance.

The Bug Recyclers was illustrated by Patricia Gibson, Nathan Rose and Robyn Bailey.

The Great Rainbow Trout Escape was illustrated by Patricia Gibson and Robyn Bailey.

D is for Detecting was illustrated by Patricia Gibson and Robyn Bailey.

The Dragon-mouse was illustrated by Robyn Bailey and Patricia Gibson.

Enchanted Forest was illustrated by Nathan Rose.

The Twisted Meadow was illustrated by Robyn Bailey, Georgia Miller and Poppy McCreary.

Food thief was illustrated by Monometsi Adamson.

…And finally, *Gracie the Great* was illustrated by Robyn Bailey.

The story so far...

Our short story competition first came into being in 2019 as an idea to support World Book Day.

Simon Berry is an Optometrist with his own Independent Practice in Gilesgate. He is very keen that his Practice is part of the community and supports local causes. It was a member of his team, Bethany, who first suggested a short story competition.

Simon got ambitious and came up with a grand plan. He decided to self-publish a book with the winning entries. He wanted to start a new annual story competition. Each year the subject of the challenge would change and would raise money for different local charities.

The whole point of the Gilesgate Story Challenge is to get children excited about writing stories.

The first year, 2019, we asked for stories about eyes or glasses. All proceeds were given to Grace House Short Break and Respite (of which Simon was a Trustee.) The first year raised just under £3000. These books have now all sold out.

The second year, 2020, was the year of the pandemic. We asked for stories about Random Acts of Kindness. It was a difficult year but we still managed to raise c. £1500 that was split between The Cheesy Waffles Project and RT Projects. These charities are based in Gilesgate. At the time of writing there are still a few books available

2021 is the third year of the competition.

We would like this competition to become an annual event but it needs more support and promotion.

If you would like to help us please get in touch at

simon@simonberry.co.uk

Help us grow...

We need your help for our competition to become bigger and better each year.

Search for us online:

www.TheGilesgateStoryChallenge.com

Like us on Facebook and Instagram:

@gilesgatestorychallenge

Share our tweets:

@gilesgatestory1

But mostly - tell all your friends to buy the book!